BENNY LINDELAUF

TORTOT

THE COLD FISH WHO LOST HIS WORLD AND FOUND HIS HEART

ILLUSTRATED BY LUDWIG VOLBEDA
TRANSLATED BY LAURA WATKINSON

Pushkin Press
71–75 Shelton Street
London, WC2H 9JQ

Tortot, The Cold Fish Who Lost His World and Found His Heart was first published as
Hoe Tortot zijn vissenhart verloor in Amsterdam, 2016

First published by Pushkin Press in 2017

**Nederlands letterenfonds
dutch foundation
for literature**

This publication has been made possible with financial support
from the Dutch Foundation for Literature

10 9 8 7 6 5 4 3 2 1

ISBN 13 978 1 782691 54 9

Typeset by Tetragon, London
Printing and finishing by Wilco Books and Magazines / The Netherlands

www.pushkinpress.com

Herbs, herbs,
so green and so good,
flourishing, nourishing,
grow as you should.
Stretch out your shoots,
push down your roots.
Flourish and swell,
nourish us well.
Herbs, herbs,
so good and so green,
nourishing, flourishing,
the finest I've seen.
Herbs, herbs,
please grow like spring,
thrive, look alive,
and make my heart sing.

CONTENTS

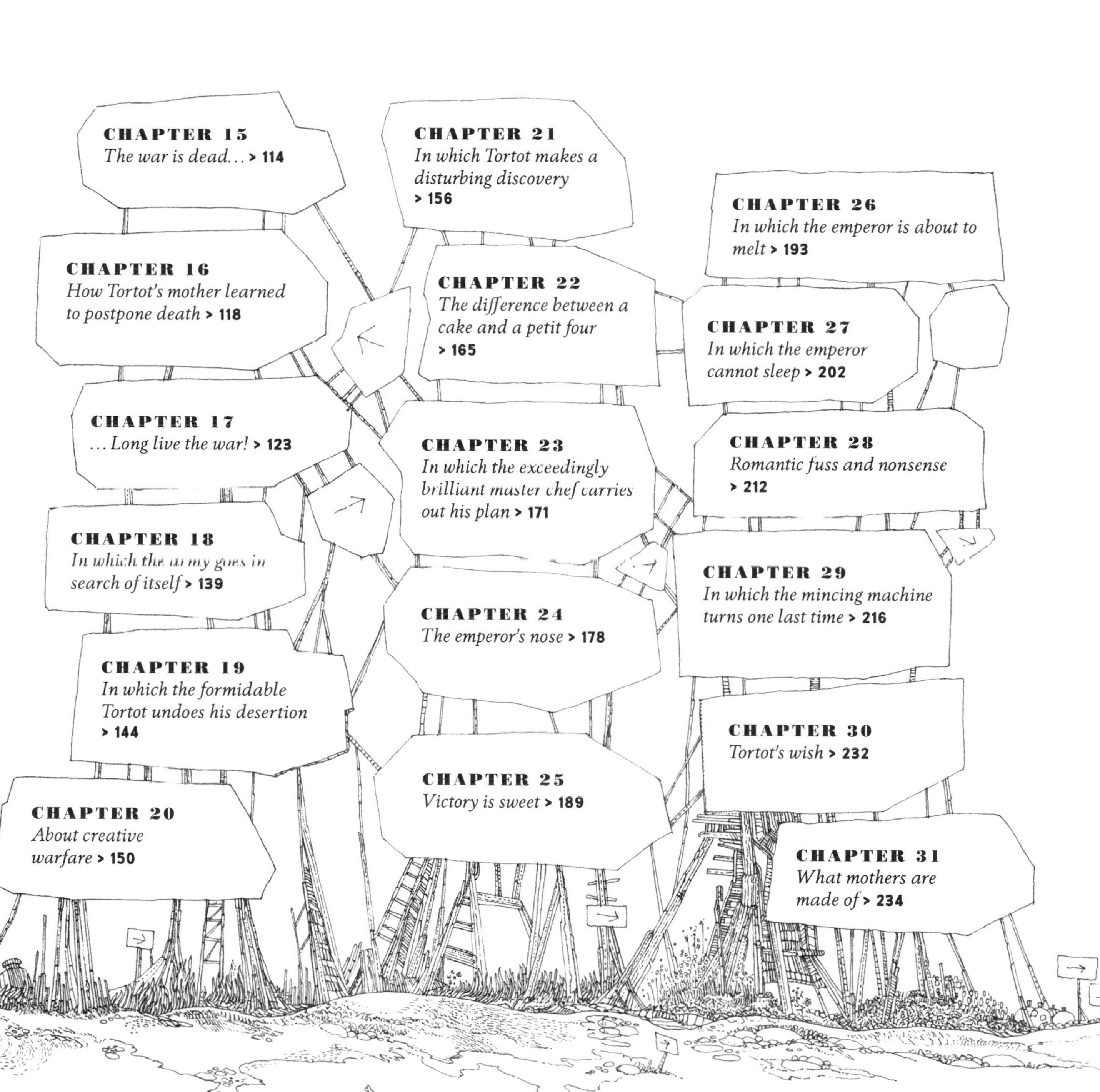

CAMP
LOUNGING LAWN

CHAPTER 1

In which the kind-hearted Tortot shows someone the way and makes a friend for life

In the days of the Great Wars, there was a field cook who travelled along with the army to all of the battles. People said Tortot had the heart of a fish at the bottom of the ocean: ice-cold and calculating. Those qualities served him well, as he lived in an age when friend and foe changed more frequently than hat fashions in Paris.

For Tortot, war was a good and generous employer. Where there was war, there were soldiers who needed to be fed. As far as he was concerned, the fighting could go on for ever.

One morning, a new company arrived at the camp where Tortot was working. They were young men, marching neatly in step behind the buglers and the drummers. The last in line was the youngest. His smooth complexion reminded Tortot of a blancmange, fresh from the mould. The boy halted. Tortot ignored him, but the boy waited patiently.

"What do you want?" asked Tortot.

"Have you seen my brothers by any chance, sir?"

"Your brothers?"

"I heard they're serving in this army."

"And how should I know if your brothers are here?"

"They look like me, sir."

"So they've got two eyes, two ears and a nose, eh?" asked Tortot, who was plucking a partridge.

The boy looked at him in surprise. "Doesn't everyone?"

"Not here!" Tortot cried triumphantly. "Men like that are a rarity around here. We have soldiers with one eye and a nose, and soldiers with one ear and two eyes. We've even got one with two noses, but that's because the surgeon was drunk. Now that I come to think about it though..."

"Yes, sir?"

"Yes, I have seen your brothers."

"Really?"

"Yes. On the Lounging Lawn."

"The Lounging Lawn?"

"Yes, straight through the camp, left after the birch wood, right at the dead oak and then over the river."

As Tortot told him to hurry, the boy called back over his shoulder, "Sir... you've made a friend for life. George is my name. George—don't forget it, sir." He dragged his feet a little as he walked. Only now did the field cook notice that the boy was wearing expensive boots that were too big for him.

Tortot plucked the partridge until it was as naked as a new-born baby.

"Cook!"

The camp sergeant came marching up to him. "Have you seen a soldier? I'm missing one from the new company."

"Wet behind the ears? As daft as a brush?"

"Exactly."

"He's gone to the graveyard," said Tortot without glancing up. "He's looking for his brothers. Or what's left of them."

Left ear
Right ear
Left eye
Right eye
Nose
ft ear
ght ear
ft eye
ght eye
ose
Left ear
Right ear
Left eye
Right eye
Nose
Left ear
Right ear
Left eye
Right eye
Nose X
Left ear
Right ear X
Left eye
Right eye
Nose

CHAPTER 2

In which the steadfast field cook proves his undying loyalty

That week, a new battle was fought. In those days, the time and place were agreed well in advance. This was not simply a question of courtesy; war was an expensive business, and time was money. If both armies first had to find each other before they could attack...

Most of the men perished like mayflies, forgetting all of their orders and strategies as soon as they were on the battlefield, some of them dying with a grin on their faces. For anyone who still had legs to walk back with, there were mugs of beer and a feast like Christmas dinner waiting at the camp.

And while the surgeon sewed the soldiers together again, with parts that sometimes belonged to the victim and sometimes did not, the generals devised new strategies on their maps, which bristled with pins.

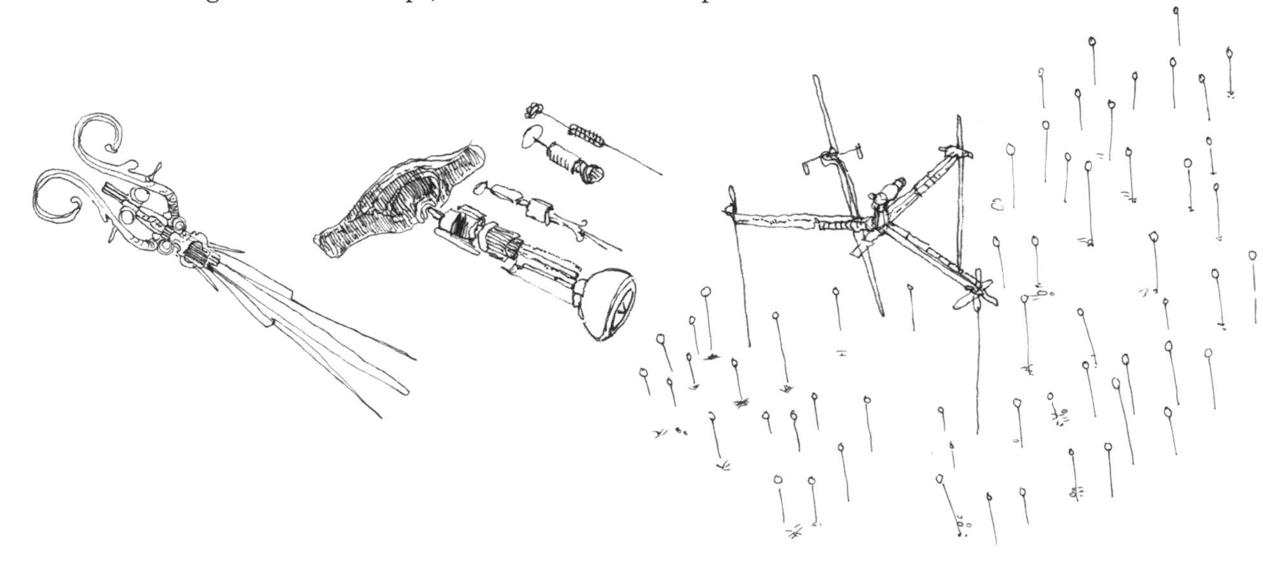

As the week progressed, the almost jolly atmosphere of the battlefield inevitably gave way to a grim conflict. Everyone who still had hands or feet (not necessarily both) was carried or pushed or, if needs be, rolled back onto the battlefield. And the battle song rang out all around:

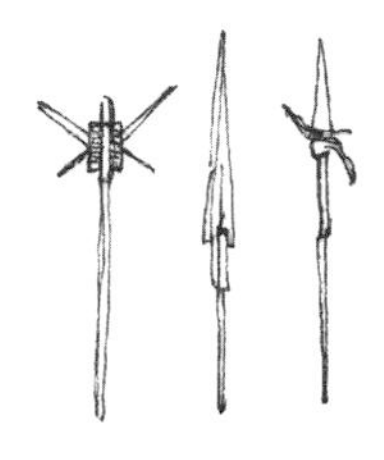
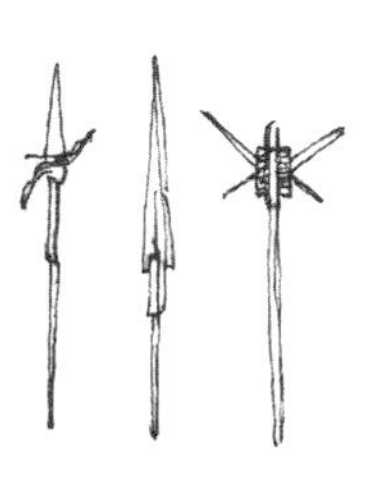

Hack, hack, hack,
chop the foe into the pot!
Whack, whack, whack,
let's cook him nice and hot!
Mash, mash, mash,
beat him up until he's dead!
Bash, bash, bash,
grind his bones to make my bread!
He is weak, we are strong,
and we sing a hero's song.
Hack, whack, bash, mash!
Hack, whack, bash, mash!
Wham! Bam! Dead!

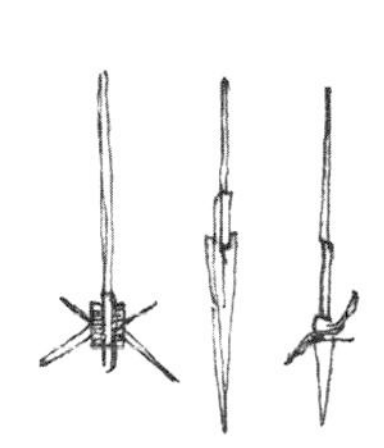
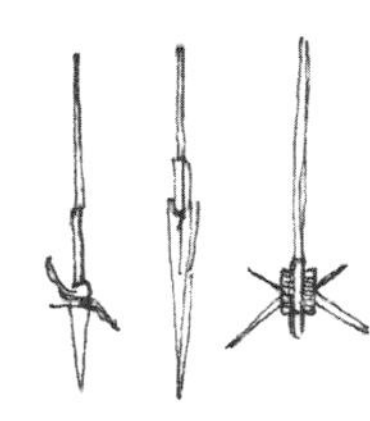

In his many years as a field cook, Tortot had developed an uncanny intuition. That night, he secretly took down his tent. He loaded up his bespectacled donkey with the tent, his pots and pans, and his flask of Eternal Soup. Then he headed into the night, past the drowsing guards. Straight into the enemy camp.

Was his heart almost pounding out of his chest?

Was there sweat upon his brow?

Of course not. Even as he walked towards them, his white apron and chef's hat announcing his approach from a distance of a hundred yards, *even* when the enemy army seized him roughly and dragged him to the scaffold and put his head on the chopping block, his heart was beating as calmly as the heart of a sleeping stingray.

"I have a right to one last request," said Tortot.

"Balderdash," said the sergeant who was holding him on the scaffold. His name was Nilliewasser, but the other men knew him as Crookleg. "Off with his head."

"It says so in the handbook," said Tortot.

"Which handbook?"

"*The Etiquette of Warfare*."

"Nonsense! Off with his head!"

When the soldier hesitated, Crookleg pushed him away and raised the blade himself. A few of the soldiers began to object. They intended to respect *The Etiquette of Warfare*, even though they were not entirely certain it existed. No one wanted to be accused of mutiny!

The situation escalated when the major caught wind of the imminent execution. He boxed the sergeant about the ears. Had Nilliewasser been born that stupid or had his brain shrivelled as he got older? What kind of idiot ignores military protocol?

"Sorry, brother," said Crookleg.

That earned him another box about the ears.

The Nilliewasser brothers came from a military family. Great-grandfather Nilliewasser had started out as a chicken farmer. His ambition reached beyond that, but he had no money to study. So, instead, he focused his scientific interests on his chickens. He carried out new experiments every week. On one occasion, he gave all the chickens oats, except for one old and balding hen who was ignored by the rooster and the other chickens—until Great-grandfather Nilliewasser began feeding her with pieces of bread and sugar. He also gave the sugared bread to whichever chicken was strutting around closest to the old hen. When the

XXX

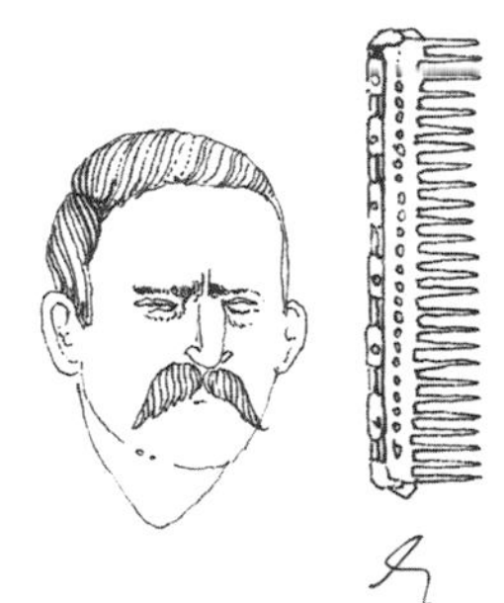

THE ETIQUETTE
OF WARFARE

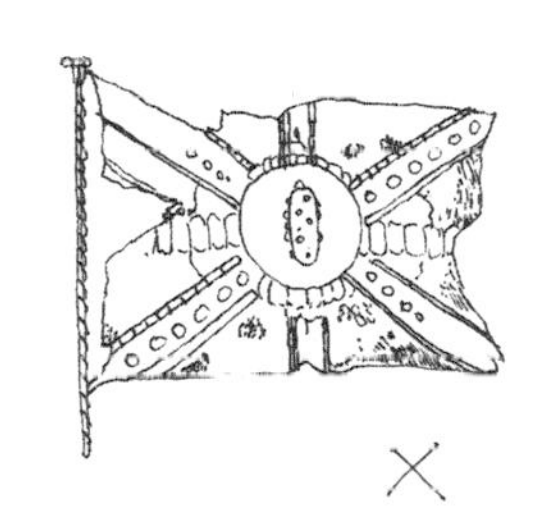

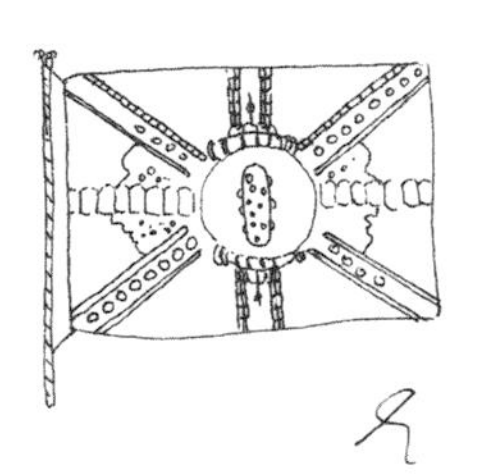

chickens realized what was happening, the hen's popularity soared. The other chickens crowded around, almost crushing her. The only hen that the rooster wanted to mount was that one, much to the poor, bewildered creature's alarm.

Another time, he split the group in two. Every day for a month, he gave one half all the fresh water they wanted, while the other half had to make do with a single cup of ditch water. The result was a phenomenal chicken war between the two camps, involving all manner of cunning plots. There was spying, collaboration, intimidation and even assassination.

Great-grandfather Nilliewasser's years of research could well explain his astounding skill for strategy when, after a long period of peace, a new war broke out. As there were very few war schools or military academies in those days, and soldiers learned about war largely through practical experience, Great-grandfather Nilliewasser, also known as the Chicken King, climbed the ranks to colonel in no time.

This set the bar high for future generations of Nilliewassers.

His son, Grandfather Nilliewasser, appeared to have a military career all laid out for him. But he had the misfortune of growing up in the longest period of peace in history. By the time he could finally go to war, he was forty-seven years old. Sadly, though, he was promoted to eternal glory on his very first day of battle, as he ducked under his horse to fasten its girth. At that very moment, the animal suffered an epileptic fit, fell to the ground and crushed Grandfather Nilliewasser's head.

Father Nilliewasser narrowly succeeded in saving the family honour by winning the key battle in a rather significant war. The wildest and most gruesome rumours about that victory flew around, unfairly earning the man a reputation as a great warrior. In truth, all it had taken was a set of poker cards, as the recently promoted colonel had trumped the enemy with a royal flush.

Nilliewasser the Poker Player had two sons. The elder son was destined to become the first general in the Nilliewasser family. By the age of two, the child already had a military uniform, a custom-made mini-musket that actually fired, and a pony that knew every military command, including how to play dead, how to carry secret messages in its mouth and how to trample the enemy under its teacup-sized hoofs.

But when he had just turned sixteen (the son, not the pony) and was about to leave for the military academy, the boy was found to be suffering from a growth disorder in his left leg. It did not merely cease to grow from that day on, but shrank by a quarter of an inch every year.

Even after Crookleg was given his very first boot with a granite heel (to compensate for the difference between the two legs), the academy refused to accept him. The colonel's sure-fire successor was unceremoniously packed off to the local war school, an institution that was considered a dumping ground for every reject with military ambitions.

For his father, Nilliewasser the Poker Player, the chapter was quickly closed.

A year later, the second son, Nilliewasser the Fair, also known as Fairface, was sent to the military academy in his brother's place.

The soldiers behind Crookleg sniggered. The sergeant turned bright red.

"And all I asked for was one last request," said Tortot cunningly.

"Which is?" asked Fairface.

"One last meal."

A cry of dismay went through the crowd. The unspoken agreement between the condemned man and the army was that the last request should be enjoyable for both parties. Where was the fun in watching someone eat?

"What do you want to eat?" Fairface asked in a weary voice.

With some difficulty, Tortot turned his head on the block. "Nothing."

It wouldn't be the first time, thought the major, *that a condemned man lost his mind when staring death in the face...*

"Nothing?"

NILLIEWASSER

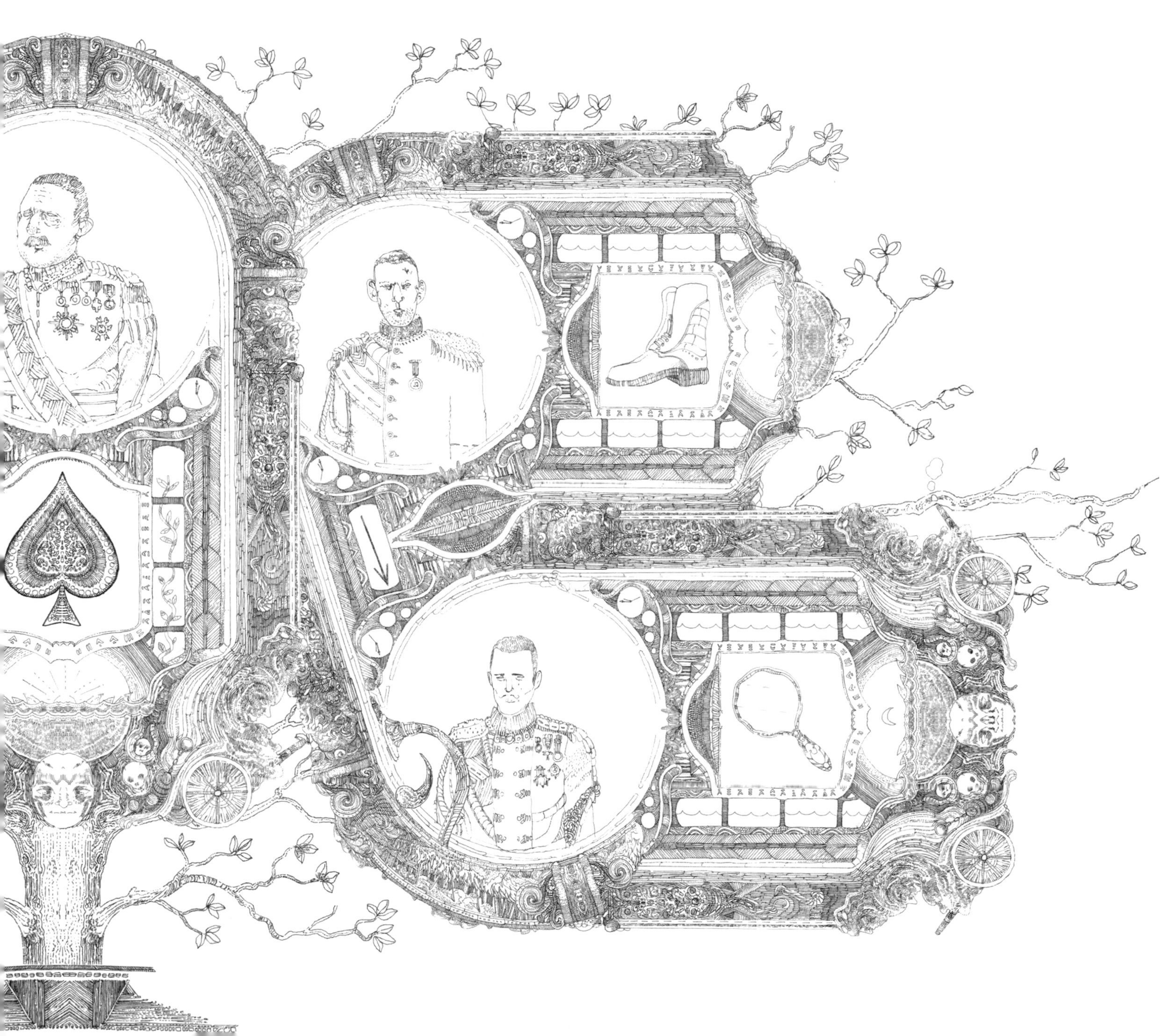

"My last wish is to *cook* one more time," said Tortot. "Before I go to meet my dear departed mother once again in Our Father's Heavenly Kingdom, I would like to prepare one final meal—for your army. It would be a great honour."

Now this enemy officer may not have been much brighter than most other military men, but that did not mean he was a fool.

"To cook for us? Fine," said Fairface. "But don't get any bright ideas. If you want to poison us, you'll have to suffer the consequences, too. You'll take the first taste of every dish."

But not a single cell of Tortot's brain was even contemplating such an idea. Yes, he had a dozen different sorts of poisons under his chef's hat, but he only used them in the last resort.

He was going to cook for the enemy army.

And could Tortot cook?

Can a fish swim?

If you gave Tortot two cows' eyes, a dried-up onion, a limp carrot and the marrow of a skinned cat, he would turn them into a soup that was reminiscent of Breton fish stew, with a full and rich flavour, a soup that took so long to digest that you would still be doing aromatic belches three days later, which were so nutritious that they alone would keep you going for another two days. If you gave Tortot the bones of a wood pigeon, he would boil them to make gelatine, add the juice of a beetroot, pour it into a double mould and press a crimson cranberry into the top of each flesh-coloured mound. This trembling pudding would make you believe you were in the red-light district in Paris, where such cheeky and frivolous delicacies were displayed in the windows of many a *pâtisserie*.

Less than three hours later, the most delicious scents were wafting over the camp. Greedy soldiers stormed Tortot's small tent, jostling and crowding around.

The order for Tortot to taste the food himself first? Forgotten.

The fact that the cook belonged to the enemy army? Forgotten.

"You must put yourself at the disposal of our army *at once*," declared Nilliewasser the Fair after licking his plate clean (both sides). "From now on you shall cook for the senior ranks."

Now any cook—anyone in such tricky circumstances, in fact—would count himself lucky to hear those words, but not Tortot. "I'd rather choose death!" he cried. Before anyone could stop him, he raced to the scaffold and put his head back on the block. "My loyalty is to my own army alone!"

"You'll be well paid!"

"Loyalty is not for sale."

"One piece of silver."

"You insult me!"

"Three pieces of silver."

"Nothing worldly can tempt me!" Tortot pulled his head out of the hole. "I want to meet my poor old mother in the Heavenly Kingdom again. That is all."

"We have no say over what happens in that kingdom," barked the major.

"But I've lived a life of sin. I'll go to hell!"

"War is everywhere these days, so hell is already full to bursting."

"Colonel! My poor old mother will die a thousand deaths if she looks down from that celestial blue kingdom, where she is seated beside God, and sees me burning in hell."

Nilliewasser the Fair (rather pleased to have been taken for a colonel) said, "Go on."

"I will only live in peace if I can pay the price for my guilty soul."

"I understand. How many pieces of silver? Four, five?"

"One hundred."

"ONE HUNDRED?"

"My life was very sinful indeed."

"I'm sorry. That's impossible."

Sobbing, Tortot cried out, "Farewell, world! My dear mother in heaven, the dearest mother there ever was, I am on my way to you!" And he began tugging at the rope to set the blade in motion. It took two soldiers to stop him. (The same two soldiers who had just been holding his head on the block.)

Everyone always thinks that in times of war nothing is feared more than the enemy. But there is actually no greater terror than one's own fellow soldiers. Particularly when those soldiers are hungry. Then the fat soon hits the fire. It would not be the first time mutiny had broken out over food.

"Agreed! It's agreed!" cried Nilliewasser the Fair, wiping the sweat from his brow.

If Tortot had not been so ice-cold and calculating, he would have roared with laughter, as everything had gone exactly as he had planned.

Later, much later, when Tortot was an old man and people asked him about his experiences as a field cook at the time of the Great Wars, he said he had always served in the same army.

"The same army?"

"The same army."

"But which army was it?"

"What a stupid question!" Tortot would reply. "The army that won, of course! I always served in the army that won!"

And then he would burst out laughing, before collapsing in tears, as helpless as a child.

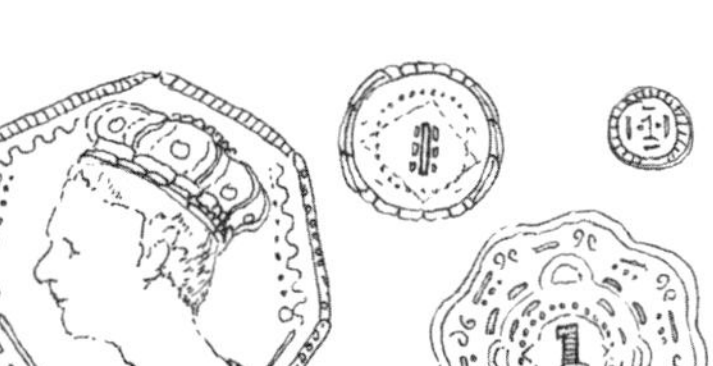

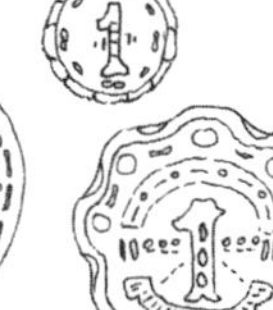
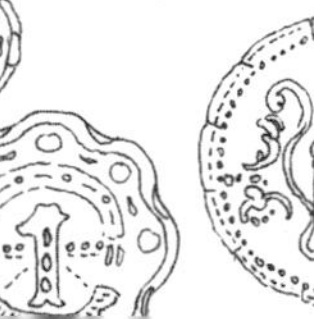

Tortot's intuition had not failed him.

The day after he left the camp, his old army was made into mincemeat.

That evening he prepared a lavish feast for the senior officers of his former enemy. He chopped, he mixed, he ground and he mashed. He conjured up soups and stews that smelled like intoxicating perfumes, he stuffed partridges and chickens until they were so very full that one careless bite could make them explode in your face. Colonel Nilliewasser, the Poker Player, who was very fond of his food, and who had already had to replace his breastplate several times because he could no longer squeeze into it, waxed lyrical about the new cook's culinary skills. Tortot was hoisted onto the men's shoulders as if he himself had won the battle. The only one who did not join in was Crookleg. He sat grumpily on an oat bin at the back of the mess tent, kicking dents in the ground with his granite heel.

The last of the officers left the tent towards dawn. They walked in single file, with their hands on the shoulders of the man in front. Whenever it looked as if the chain of officers were about to stumble off the path, the last and least drunken officer braced himself. And so they swayed from tent to tent until the final officer reached his camp bed.

Tortot was so worn out that he did not even bother to undress when he got back to his tent. He promptly fell asleep on top of his bedclothes and did not notice two nightwatchmen delivering new supplies in large wooden barrels. And when they left, they forgot to close the tent flap.

CHAPTER 3

In which the poor, tormented field cook has a dream he would rather forget

Tortot dreamed about the place where he was born. There, on the edge of the village, his little old mother lived in a crooked house surrounded by four crooked walls with sleeping lizards clinging to them. Sometimes one of them would fall off the wall with a soft, dry thud. Otherwise nothing ever happened.

Tortot dreamed about the mighty crooked oak in the middle of his mother's crooked little garden. The oak shared the sunlight among the plants, just as Tortot's mother had once shared the food among her sons. Now her herb garden was her brood. Every leaf was a child. She gathered them in her bunched-up apron, one by one, and sang as she rocked them, just as she had once rocked her sons:

Herbs, herbs,
so green and so good,
flourishing, nourishing,
grow as you should.
Stretch out your shoots,
push down your roots.
Flourish and swell,
nourish us well.
Herbs, herbs,
so good and so green,
nourishing, flourishing,
the finest I've seen.
Herbs, herbs,
please grow like spring,
thrive, look alive,
and make my heart sing.

As the cook, in the depths of sleep, called out for his mother, a wind blew through the open tent flap, a wind from the north, a sly and ice-cold breeze, drawn to Tortot's sweaty brow.

CHAPTER 4

In which the good and honest Tortot is scandalously robbed

When Tortot awoke the next morning, his head felt hot, his throat was raw, and his nose was extremely itchy.

A cold, in itself, would not normally have been an insurmountable problem for the field cook. With a little bluffing and some bouillon, he could have got by, but then he remembered what Colonel Nilliewasser had said when he had summoned him the day before.

"Very well, Tortot," the Poker Player had said. "We will spare your life. For now. Tomorrow the Imperial Emperors are to visit the site of our victory. I assume you know who they are?"

It was a question that required no answer. Everyone knew the Imperial Emperors, the twin sons of the former Duke of Arcadia.

After the duke's death, they had assumed power of Arcadia. Unlike their father, an amiable man who lived mainly for his hunting, his lively parties and his long line of lovers, the twins' ambition knew no bounds. They did not want a duchy, but an empire to rival Caesar's.

Back then, Arcadia lay at the centre of a rich patchwork of counties, duchies and city-states. This patchwork was bordered by the sea in the east and by the mountains in the west.

During their subsequent rule of almost seventy years, they had systematically expanded their duchy, first by playing off the various neighbours against one another and entering into alliances. Later, at the time of the Great Wars, they waged aggressive battles of expansion. And they had been rather successful. Two-thirds of the patchwork was now in their hands.

But still their thirst for power had not been quenched.

"Of course I know who the Imperial Emperors are," said Tortot.

"Good," said the Poker Player, "then I'm sure I won't need to remind you about what must be on the menu."

The elderly emperors were famous for their love of pickled gherkins.

In fact, they believed they owed their beautiful smooth complexions to gherkins. (The Twin Emperors' faces were, in fact, as pockmarked as gravel pits, but no one dared to say so.)

Before every banquet, it was announced that the preparation of dishes that included plenty of gherkins *would be most appreciated*.

Which in imperial language meant: Gherkins! Or it's off with your head!

Tortot stumbled from his camp bed, walked to the herb cabinet and buried his nose in the bunch of fresh basil. Then he sniffed at the leftovers of the stew.

Finally, he took an ancient goat's cheese out from under its cover. It was a cheese that Tortot employed in minute quantities to instantly transform a hopelessly bland dish into a taste sensation. In Italy, the cheese was widely known as "Virgin Cheese". It was used when young women from remote villages were married off and had to make their way to their future husband's home. Two small lumps, pressed into the armpits, ensured that the women could walk through even the most unsavoury forests full of highwaymen without being bothered even for a second. The only drawback was that the wedding had to be postponed for a couple of months. That was how long it took for the horrendous stench to wear off.

Tortot sniffed carefully at first, holding the cheese at arm's length. Then he brought the Virgin Cheese closer, finally pushing his nose into it, which under ordinary circumstances was extremely dangerous.

Nothing.

He could smell nothing.

Tortot still did not panic. After all, he had the heart of a fish at the bottom of the ocean.

"Not being able to smell doesn't mean I can't taste anything," he said to himself. "I'll surely be able to taste a sour pickled gherkin!"

Just as he leaned forward to the barrel of gherkins, the lid came off.

A head peeped out.

"Am I past it?" asked the head.

"Sorry?"

"Am I past it?"

"Past what?" asked Tortot.

"Past the war."

Tortot took a step forward. He looked more closely at the head. Wait a moment... Didn't he recognize it? As smooth as... a blancmange, fresh from the mould! Then he remembered. It was the boy who had asked him about his brothers. That... Boris. No, Lars. No, George.

Everything about George was lean and skinny. Not just his neck and head, his arms and torso, but his nose and lips too. Even the expression on his face was thin.

"Please, sir... could you tell me if I'm past the..."

"No, you're not past the war," said Tortot gruffly. "And might I point out that you're sitting inside the Imperial Emperors' barrel of gherkins?"

"I haven't escaped?"

"You're in the enemy camp."

The boy's face went even whiter. "In the enemy camp?"

"Are you practising to be a parrot or something?"

"Am I practising?..."

"Out."

The boy looked at him helplessly.

"You're not going to tell me you're too fat, are you?" sneered Tortot. "Or too old?"

"I've just turned twelve, sir."

"Twelve already? Ah, doesn't time fly! Congratulations. I sincerely hope you had a very fine birthday. And now—scram!"

"That, erm, won't be possible."

Tortot had had enough. He leaned forward to pull the boy out of the barrel and then recoiled in horror.

In his life as a field cook, Tortot had seen quite a number of mutilated soldiers. The surgeon who had operated on the boy must have been a novice or drunk or blind, probably all three.

George was now, well... Half-George. The boy had barely any legs left. Somewhere just beneath his bottom, he stopped. And without going into detail, not very neatly. But that was not the main reason for Tortot's shock.

"My gherkins!" cried Tortot. "Where have my gherkins gone?"

"I've been inside the barrel for four days."

GREAT-GREAT-GREAT-GREAT-GREAT-GREAT-GRANDMOTHER

Tortot frowned. “You’re not telling me that...”

The boy nodded.

“You’ve eaten all of them?!”

GREAT-GREAT-GREAT-GREAT-GREAT-GRANDMOTHER

Limping footsteps approached the tent.

“Cook!”

Tortot looked at the boy and put a finger to his lips, but there was no need. Half-George’s eyes were already bulging with fear.

GREAT-GREAT-GREAT-GREAT-GRANDMOTHER

“Who’s there?” asked Tortot, even though the limping steps had given it away.

“Sergeant Nilliewasser.”

“What is it?”

“My broth... um... the major wants to know why we can’t yet smell any fine and festive cooking aromas for the Imperial Emperors’ meal.”

GREAT-GREAT-GREAT-GRANDMOTHER

It was easy enough to guess what would happen if Crookleg came in and discovered that Tortot was hiding a soldier from the enemy camp inside his gherkin barrel. If Tortot were lucky, they would behead him for high treason, but it was more likely that he would be quartered, after having been slowly boiled in his own soup pot.

GREAT-GREAT-GRANDMOTHER

The field cook did not hesitate. “Stay out of here! No outside air may touch this dish or it will all go wrong. And if that happens, I refuse to accept any responsibility whatsoever.”

“Then hurry up, cook,” said the irritable voice. “The Imperial Emperors do not like to be kept waiting.”

Crookleg hobbled away again.

Tortot walked to the middle of the tent, where the pot of Eternal Soup was standing. The soup was based on the extract his mother had given him, a small, crooked flask full.

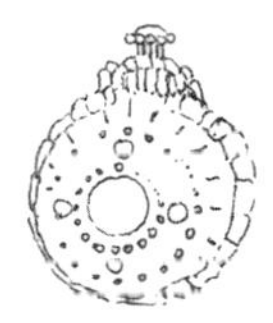

"Use this in your pot," she had said, "and make sure you never see the bottom. Whenever it looks as if the pot is about to run dry, top it up with fresh stock and whatever herbs, vegetables and meat you can find. Just as I did, and my grandmother and my great-grandmother before me. This Eternal Soup gives strength to those without strength and courage to those without courage."

Tortot tasted. He smacked his lips, ran his tongue around his mouth like a spatula, but he might as well have been drinking milky water, that was how bland the concoction tasted. He sprinkled a handful of salt in the pot and tried again.

Nothing.

So he threw in another handful of salt and had another taste.

"Sir... Sir..." Half-George's eyes came just over the edge of the barrel. They were glistening like lumps of wet coal.

"What?"

"Shall I?..."

"Clear off!" growled Tortot.

Once again, Crookleg's footsteps approached the tent.

"Cook!"

"Yes?"

"The major wishes to inform you that the coach of the Twin Emperors has been sighted, five hours' march away."

"That's nice," replied Tortot. "Now leave me in peace. I need to concentrate. If this meal goes wrong, I will show no mercy to the person who kept coming to disturb me."

The sergeant disappeared, muttering to himself.

In the silence that followed, Tortot stared angrily at Half-George. Then he held out the spoonful of soup.

Half-George tasted the soup without hesitation.

His eyes widened.

He screwed up his mouth.

He spat it back out.

Tortot grasped the boy by his skinny neck. "Too bitter? Too bland? What is it? Tell me!"

"Too s-salty," stammered Half-George. "That soup is saltier than the sea."

It was an incredible gamble. Half-George's taste buds were most likely as unsophisticated as the average yokel's, but what else could he do? Tortot had no choice. Without any gherkins, his hours were numbered.

How exactly the cook with the fish's heart finally succeeded, with Half-George's assistance, in preparing a seven-course meal in which every dish had the sweetly sour taste and the slippery texture of gherkins, without using even one single gherkin—that will always remain a secret.

"I'd swear there are gherkins in it," said Half-George, flabbergasted.
"The proof of the pudding is in the eating," said Tortot, nodding sagely.

The Imperial Emperors arrived in the late afternoon, in an open-top carriage with a linen canopy to protect them from the sun. Cries of admiration filled the air. The officers' wives sobbed and clutched at their bosoms; the ladies of pleasure, in all their finery, hummed and buzzed like bees in a hive. The whole camp went wild.

"Long live our youthful emperors!"

"Such strength!"

"What agility!"

"May our sons be as handsome as them!"

The fact that it was all lies did nothing to diminish the enthusiastic praise for the beauty of the Imperial Emperors.

Because, of course, before every visit, it was announced that a warm welcome from the entire camp *would be most appreciated*.

Which in imperial language meant: Lie your head off! Or we'll chop it off for you!

In their younger years, the Imperial Emperors had been so stunning that people sometimes turned away when they saw them, as if they had been slapped in the face.

One evening, though, when they had just turned fourteen, they were out hunting with a patrol in the ducal forests around the castle and became lost. When it started raining, the mood of the duke's sons sank to below zero. Soaked through, they came to a remote hut.

Inside, where a smouldering fire was the only source of light, a girl sat wrapped in a blanket, holding a baby. The child would not stop wailing, so the guards chased them both outside, into the night. Then the twins snuggled up

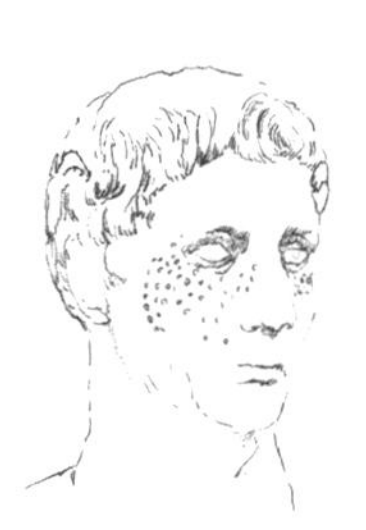

in the blanket. They had an excellent night's sleep, because even though the bed was made of straw, it was fresh and had been made with love.

The next day, the duke's sons awoke early. The rain had stopped. One of them went outside to the nearby spring. The girl sat there shivering with her baby, beside a feeble fire. He ignored her and quenched his thirst. She did not look up at him until he went to warm himself by her fire, suddenly feeling strangely shy. That was when he saw that her face was disfigured by scars.

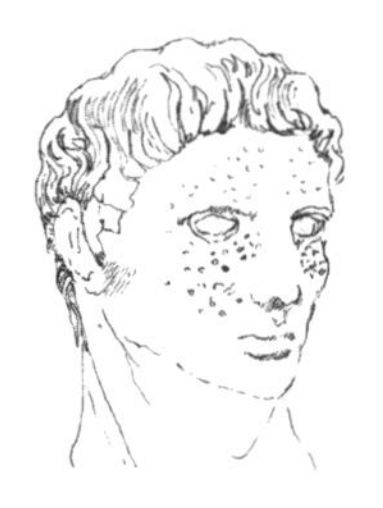

But that was not the worst of it.

The baby in her arms was covered in scabs like scales.

"A fish's child!" he said, howling with laughter, when they were finally at home and it all seemed like a bad dream. "She'd given birth to a fish's child!"

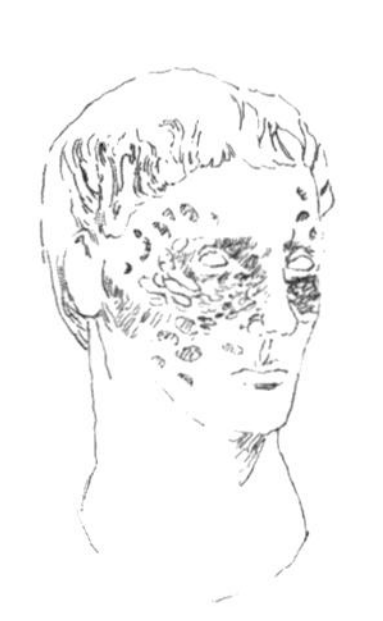

Two days later, the twins developed fevers, so high that the doctors feared for their lives. After a fortnight, hard blisters like goat droppings swelled first on their bodies, then on their faces.

The itching and the pain were so severe that their parents had them put into straitjackets to stop them scratching and breaking their skin open. Then, a week later, a cloudy, pus-like fluid came trickling out of the blisters. This dried to form scabs that flaked so badly that everyone thought nothing would be left of the Twin Emperors.

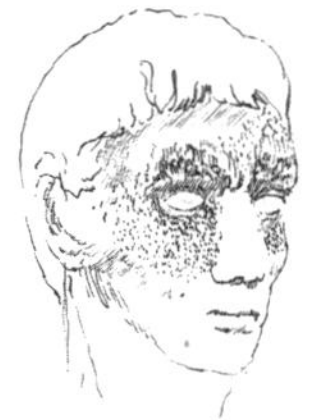

During their illness, the twins' mother and father had kept the boys separated with a folding screen. All the mirrors were removed. But no one had remembered that twins do not

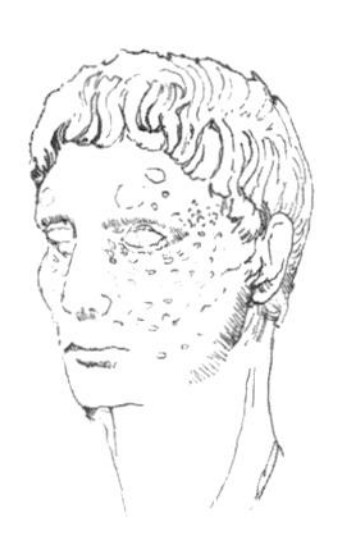

need a mirror to see themselves. One morning, on the first day when they did not feel entirely sick and wretched, they pushed aside the screen.

The shouts and screams reached even the most distant of the thirty-four rooms in that wing.

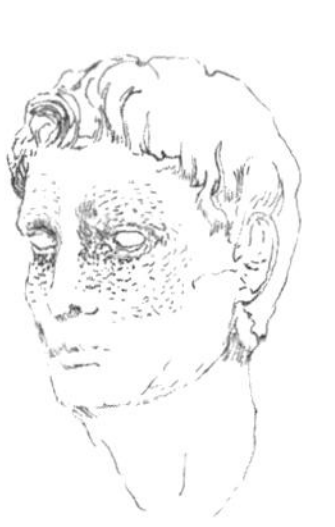

A few years before that, on their eleventh birthday, the twins had been given a life-sized ceramic bust of Emperor Caesar. Later that day, when they were in their playroom, an argument had broken out about who should have the emperor when they were grown up.

In the heated fight that followed, the bust fell to the floor and shattered into dozens of pieces. When their father found out what had happened, he forced them to patch up their quarrel. And they were not allowed to go to their birthday party until they had mended the emperor.

The boys had furiously gathered up the pieces.

The result was not just pitiful, but terrifying. Much of the gold leaf that covered the bust had cracked and fallen off. There was red clay beneath, so it looked as if the emperor's face were bleeding. The left and right eyes had been swapped, which gave him a rather sinister expression.

And the nose was never found. There was just a gaping hole.

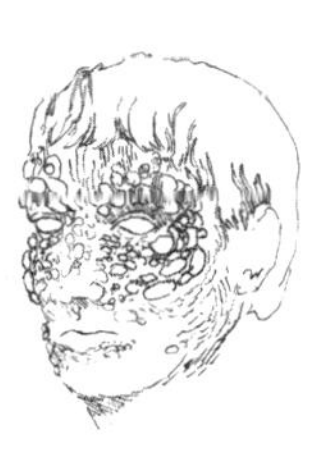

The result was so monstrous that it gave the boys nightmares. Not long after that, the bust was taken away. But when, three years later, having narrowly survived smallpox, they pushed aside the screen and saw each other, it was as if the monster emperor had somehow risen from the depths of the cellar and was staring them right in the face.

Surgeons and scientists were summoned. They tried with all their might to restore the boys' handsome looks. Some prescribed compresses of calves' blood and tincture of marigold. Others swore by bloodletting or leeches, but nothing helped.

Not long after that, the twins' mother woke up with a spot on her left arm. She died less than two weeks later. Their father hung on for another month.

At the age of fifteen, the twins became dukes.

There are many stories about how the gherkins came into the Imperial Emperors' lives, each more far-fetched than the next, but the following is the most likely account. During one of their first military campaigns, the young dukes met a peasant girl with a complexion as smooth and perfect as a tomato's skin. They ordered her to reveal her beauty secret. The simple girl (who, to be honest, was not particularly bright) had no reply for them, so her parents boxed her about the ears.

"Tell them!" they cried in panic. "Don't make the gentlemen wait!" And they pulled her plaits, they pinched her black and blue, but all the girl could do was sob and snivel. And so the parents came up with a story on the spot: they said that, since her birth, their daughter had eaten only gherkins.

"She *eats* them?" the twins asked sceptically. "That's all?"

And the parents, who scarcely dared to look up at the furious and monstrously disfigured faces of the two young dukes and at the soldiers' bayonets, which they felt jabbing into their backs, quickly added that she put mashed gherkin on her face. Every single day.

The girl fetched some gherkins from the field and trembled as she boiled them to make a hot, slimy mush, which she then spread on the twins' faces. And when she removed the sludge an hour later, she was so frightened that she not only imagined they looked better—no, she really saw it. It was as powerful as a divine vision. As if their faces were glowing with a light that came from within. The twins had never been so handsome. Crying with relief, she fell to her knees. And the dukes looked at the parents, and they could suddenly see it too, and then they looked at the soldiers and they nodded, yes, yes, incredible, it was really true, a genuine miracle, because ducal displeasure was dangerous and, with two dukes, it was doubly dangerous.

And, with the help of the soldiers' bayonets, everyone witnessed the miracle from that day on.

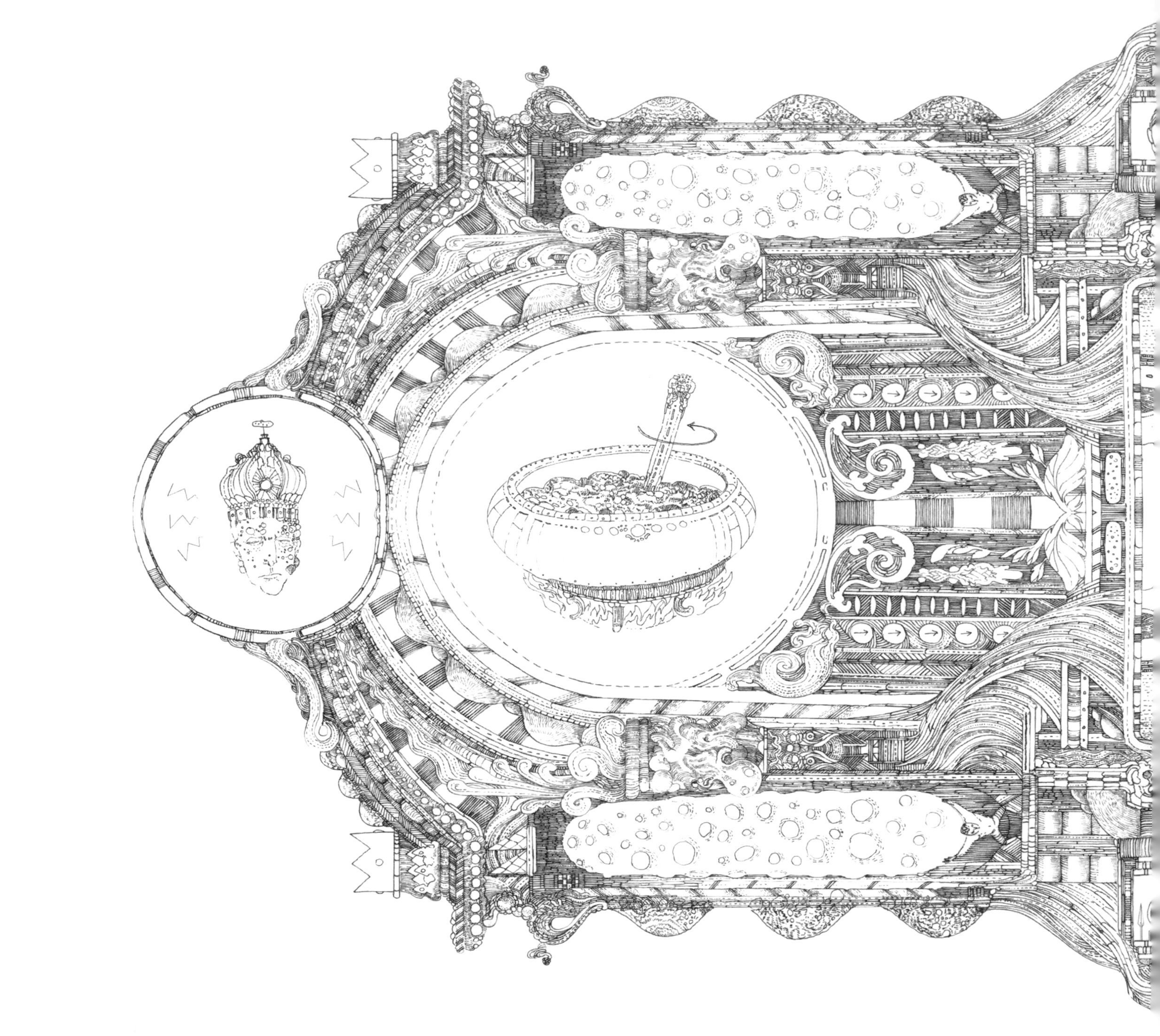

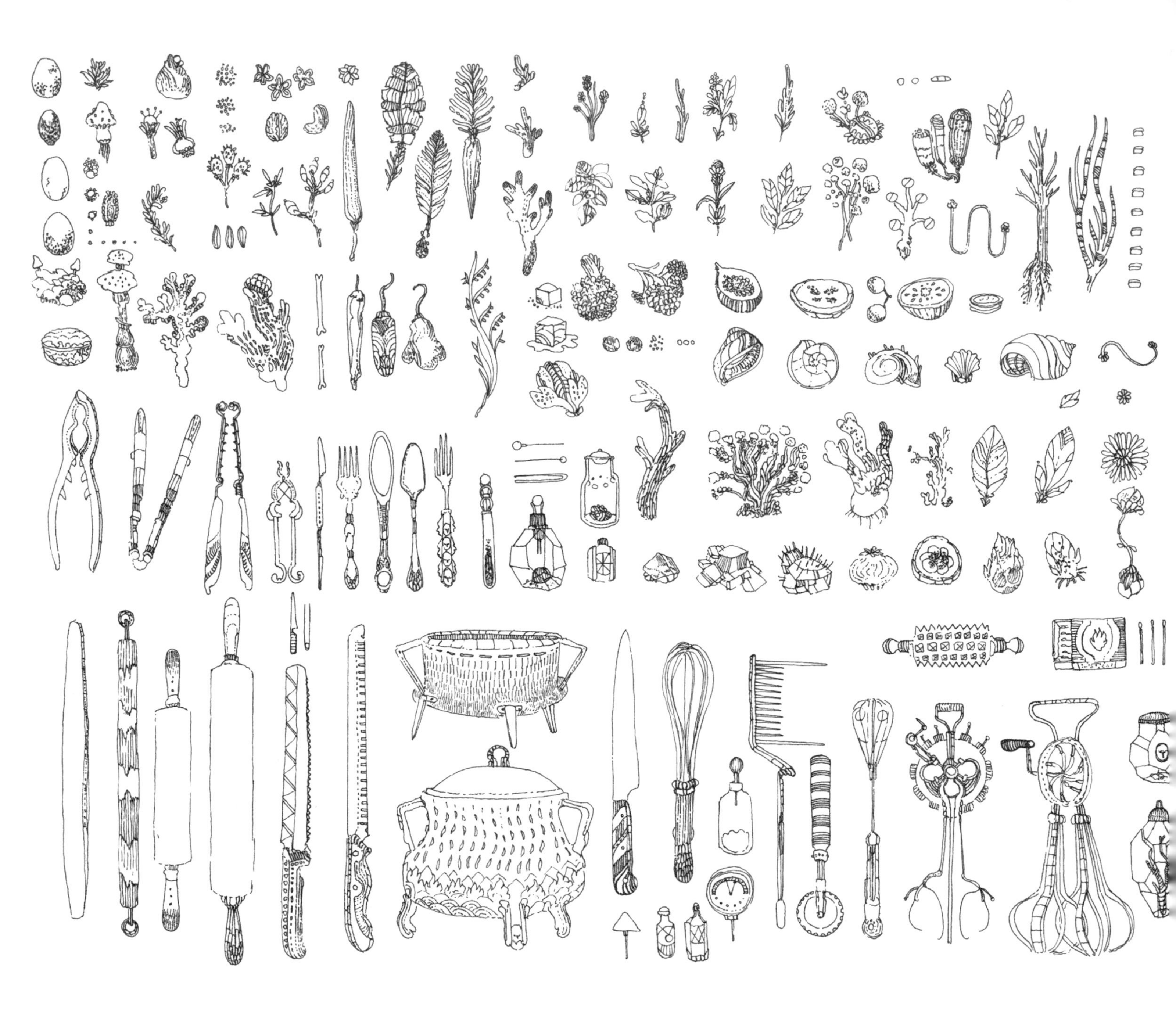

CHAPTER 5

In which no one considers that sometimes a cook wants a quiet night's sleep too

That evening, after the soldiers had fetched the meal for the Imperial Emperors, Tortot scrubbed his pots and pans. He carefully greased them with a mixture of sunflower oil and lard. He patted his wooden spatulas dry and folded oiled paper around them to protect them from damp. He arranged the herbs in his herb cabinet, wrapping each sprig of leaves in moist, cool cloth. He sanded his chopping boards until they were as smooth as babies' buttocks. When he finally bent to empty the oven's ash pan, his head was pounding with fever.

All that time he could feel Half-George's thin gaze on him. "Do you really think they'll believe there are gherkins in it?"

"Let's keep our fingers crossed," Tortot said grimly. "Or you'll be saying goodbye to your head as well as your legs."

"It went well though, didn't it?"

"What?"

"Me tasting everything."

"Any idiot can taste."

"I can grind and mix too."

"Don't go getting any ideas."

"Most cooks have assistants."

"I'm not most cooks."

"I bet I could..."

"Listen," Tortot snapped at him. "Maybe you got a bit too close to the cannons, but I DO NOT NEED ANYONE TO HELP ME. And certainly not an imbecile who was stupid enough to get his legs shot off in his first battle."

Then they heard cheering and applause in the distance.
"Tortot! Tortot!" went the chant.
"It looks like we live to cook another day," Tortot said dryly.

The field cook tucked himself in by the flickering light of the paraffin lamp, with two hot-water bottles, one on either side of him in his camp bed, a cosy blanket, his nightcap and a thick woollen scarf around his neck.

The tidy field kitchen, with every pot and every pan polished to a gleam and in the right place, always gave Tortot a feeling of calm. When it was in full swing, the kitchen was the gate to hell. A hell of fire, hot steam and hissing, bubbling pans. Now it lay there quietly like a sleeping dragon. It made Tortot drowsy, in spite of his pounding head.

"Sir?"

Tortot put his hands over his ears. All he needed was one night's sleep. Tomorrow his head would be clear again.

"Sir?"

The voice seeped in like syrup.

"What?"

"It's so cold and dark."

"It's called night."

"Will you tell me a story?"

"No."

"Can I come and lie next to you?"

"Sorry?"

"Your bed's big enough."

"For me, yes."

"I don't take up much room."

Tortot sat up and adjusted his nightcap. "Listen, squib, I didn't ask you to climb into a barrel. I didn't ask you to eat up all the Imperial Emperors' gherkins.

And besides, I have enough trouble with my own fleas. So I would very much appreciate it if you would stop your whining."

He lay back down. It was silent for a while. Until a strange shivering sound came from the barrel.

Tortot groaned. "Stop that."

"I... I... c... c... can't... h-h-help it."

The field cook jerked upright. And promptly had a fit of sneezing. With one hand pressed to his hot, aching forehead, he got up, strode to the laundry basket, fished out a dirty tablecloth, stomped back to the boy's barrel and threw the tablecloth at him.

"Make sure you're gone before daylight tomorrow. If you're still here, then on your sorry head be it!"

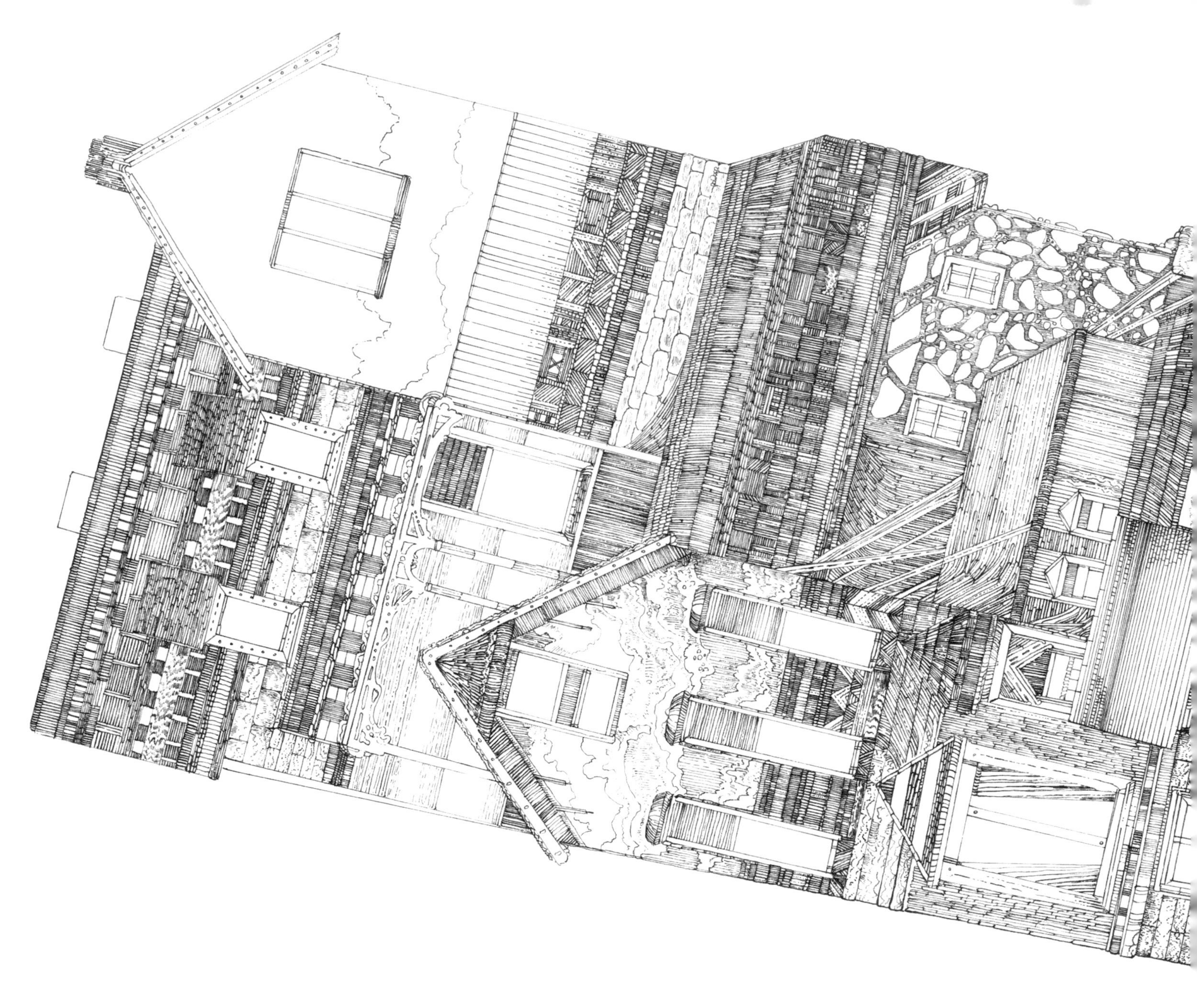

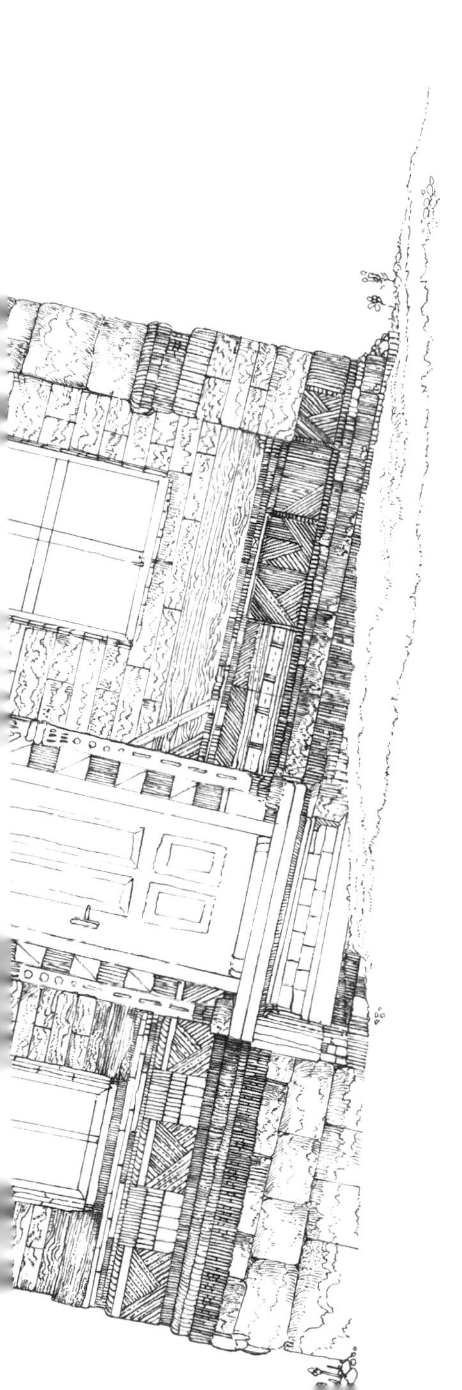

CHAPTER 6

In which the already tormented Tortot has another dream

"Bertrand, Clément, Dieudonné, Efarim, François. Dinner!"

Tortot hears his mother calling. Her voice is coming from the herb garden outside, and it carries a long way, even though it is neither deep nor loud.

"Gerard, Itrahim, Jumeaux, Tortot! Come and get it!"

His brothers' footsteps come from every direction. It is like an army thundering through the little house with its thin walls.

Tortot has hidden inside the biggest pot in the kitchen. The smooth metal feels cool against his flushed face. When he looks up, he can see the ceiling, with all the pots and pans hanging from it. At something of an odd angle, just as everything here is at an odd angle.

"Jumeaux, fetch the spoons," says Mother. "Clément and Bertrand, lay the table. Don't throw the spoons, boys. Come on, wash your hands."

Tortot wipes his tears on his sleeve. He hears Mother come into the kitchen and, even with his stuffed-up nose, he can smell what she has been picking. Basil, rosemary and thyme.

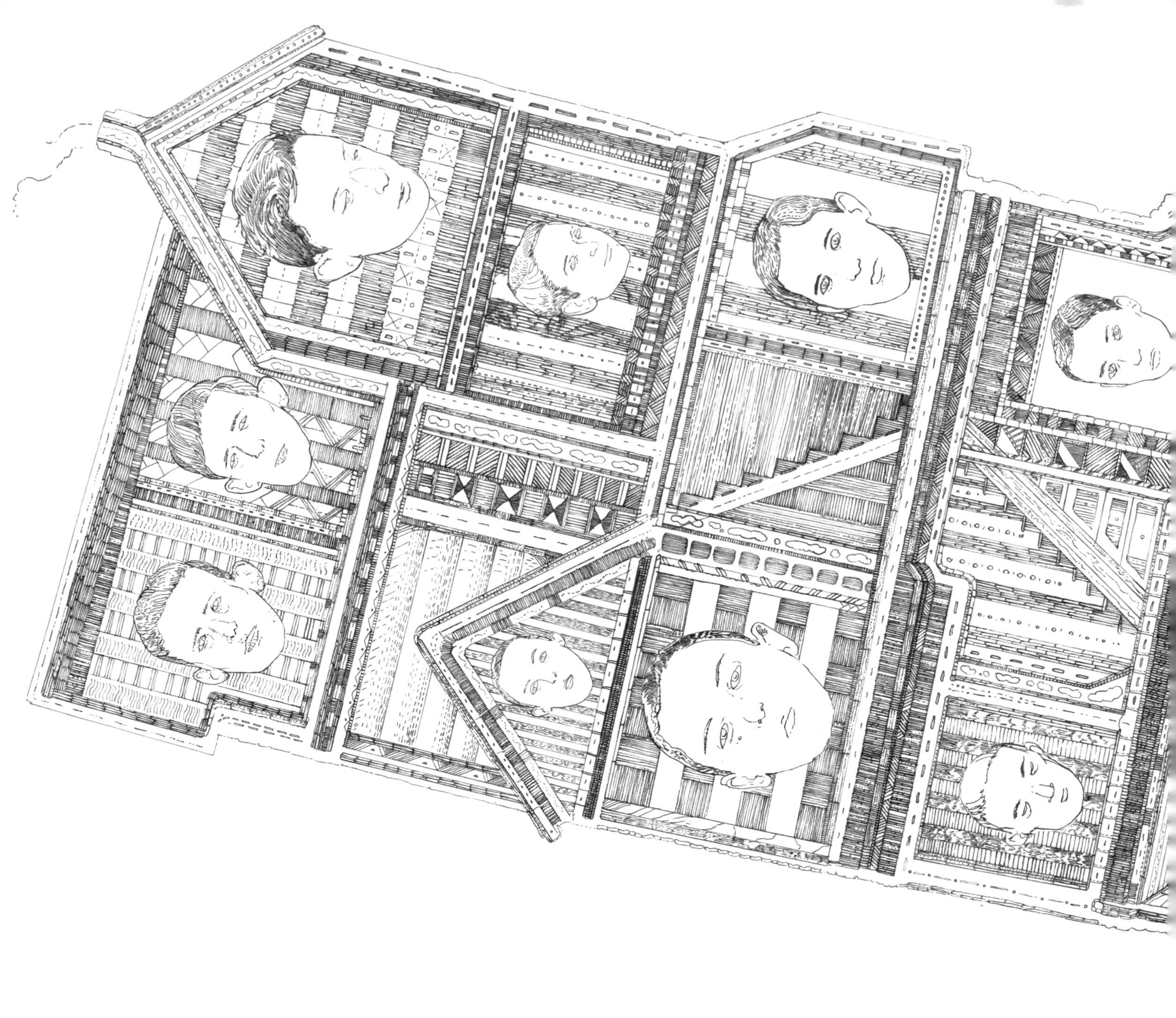

"Where's my littlest one?" she asks.

The noise and chatter instantly stop. Then it swells again, louder than before and somehow more deliberate. Tortot's mother is no fool. She can always tell when her sons have been up to something.

"Boys?"

"Mum?"

"Where's Tortot?"

There is an animated discussion. "Tortot, yes, Tortot… Hmm, where on earth could he have got to? Not in front of the house? No? Behind it? Not there either? How strange! Most peculiar! No, we haven't seen him, Mum, we were too busy doing the chores you gave us. You see the fire burning nicely? And the fence, have you seen how bright and white the fence is again?"

She lets a calculated silence fall. A silence that expands into a pit that swallows all their swagger and bravado in one gulp.

"It was just a joke…" says Itrahim in a miserable voice.

"How were we to know he'd believe the story?" asks François.

"By the time we were his age, we didn't believe anything that anyone told us," says Jumeaux.

One of the brothers had wondered how much more the Christmas rabbit would have to grow before it was too big to get out through its door. That was what had

happened to last year's Christmas rabbit—did Mum remember? When they'd had to break the whole hutch? Well, then another brother had come up with the idea of seeing if Tortot could fit through the door.

"He went in there by himself, Mum. It's not like we pushed him. We just said it was a job no one else could do. And whoosh, in he went. And, um, then we remembered the story about Antoine the Butcher."

"Antoine the Butcher?" says Mother in a suspicious voice. "What story about Antoine the Butcher?"

The brothers are suddenly a lot less eager to talk. There is plenty of coughing, though. They stare holes in the floor, but a mother is a mother. All it takes is one raised eyebrow to make her sons talk.

"Well, um, yes… Antoine. Everyone knows that before he came to live here as our village butcher, he baked the best meat pies in Badeen, don't they? And that all the bakers in Badeen were envious of his pies?"

"I have absolutely no idea what you're talking about," says Mother.

The brothers trip and stumble over one another to explain. "You know the song about Badeen, don't you, Mum? 'Badeen, Badeen, so much stone, not much green?'" And they told the story of Antoine the Butcher.

With the steep rocky slopes surrounding the town, it was difficult to keep even a herd of goats. Their meat was dry and stringy, with a sour aftertaste. So they made it into pies. You could taste the meat less when it was surrounded by a thick pastry crust.

But Antoine's pies were tender and juicy. The meat was deep red, sweet and soft as butter. The bakers suspected it was lamb, maybe veal. Did Antoine have a secret supplier? They slyly followed him, hoping he would give himself away, but they never found out anything.

And yet, every Monday, Antoine baked his pies. A hungry, eager crowd stood waiting outside his bakery. Antoine was a decent chap. He always chose a couple of young boys and invited them into the bakery, gave them a tour and sent them home with a big piece of pie.

And if every once in a while one of those boys didn't make it home after the tour, well...

It was simply a question of supply and demand. You could find boys on every corner of every street, but where could you find such delicious pies as the ones from Antoine's shop?

From the very first words of this story, Tortot put his fingers in his ears. Suddenly she is there, towering above him. Gently, she takes his fingers out of his ears.

"Oh, little one. You don't really believe that story, do you?"

Tortot feels his face twisting. He hates it when that happens, because he already knows what his brothers will soon be saying, yet again:

Cry-baby!
Wet lettuce!
Hanky-soaker!

She turns around. "Shame on you! Frightening a poor little boy like that! Just because you're big, that doesn't mean I can't still put you over my knee! Got it? Come on, Tortot. They'll never make you go in that rabbit hutch again. And they'll never tell you any silly stories about Antoine the Butcher paying good money for fresh young boys! You know Antoine, don't you? You know what he's like? He cries if he sees a lame cow limping into his slaughterhouse. Your brothers were only joking. Hey, Tortot. Come on. I'm worried about you. Come and eat. A boy of ten who can still fit inside a soup pot! What a thing!"

CHAPTER 7

In which Tortot barely manages to get his important work done, because someone keeps nagging him

A week after Half-George had turned up in the gherkin barrel, the pounding in Tortot's head had eased and the fever was almost gone, but his head was still stuffed up. He could not taste the difference between a spoonful of salt and a spoonful of sugar.

"I'm pretty handy, eh?" Half-George ventured.

Tortot threateningly stuck his nose in the air. "You know, I think my sense of smell is coming back."

But nothing could have been further from the truth. And he had to admit: even though Half-George was anything but a natural taster, he was determined and eager to learn. He sat in his barrel, tasting whatever Tortot put in front of him.

"Well?"

"Sweet."

Tortot boxed him about the ears. "Yes, even my nose understands that much! But what kind of sweet? Like the honey of the violet carpenter bee? The smoky sweetness of red peppers roasted on oak? The bitter sweetness of Prussian rock candy?"

"Um..."

Tortot gave him another slap, but of course it could have been worse. At least the boy could not get under his feet. He was as quiet as a mouse when needed. All it took was the sound of approaching footsteps, and Half-George wilted like spinach in the pan.

And yet at times he talked as if his life depended on it. Luckily, Tortot's tent was next to the armoury, a noisy place filled with clattering boots, shouted orders, and Turkish cannons screeching and squeaking as they rolled along on their wheels.

"Tortot?"

"What?"

"Do you want me to tell you how it happened?"

"How what happened?"

"How I lost my legs."

"Not interested."

"The war started at a quarter past ten, and by half past ten..."

Tortot yawned dramatically, but Half-George did not notice. "... I'd taken down two Ottovarian soldiers. Three actually, but the last one didn't really count. His bayonet was so badly bent that he ended up stabbing himself and..."

"And then you were cut down and chopped in two," said Tortot, to put an end to the story.

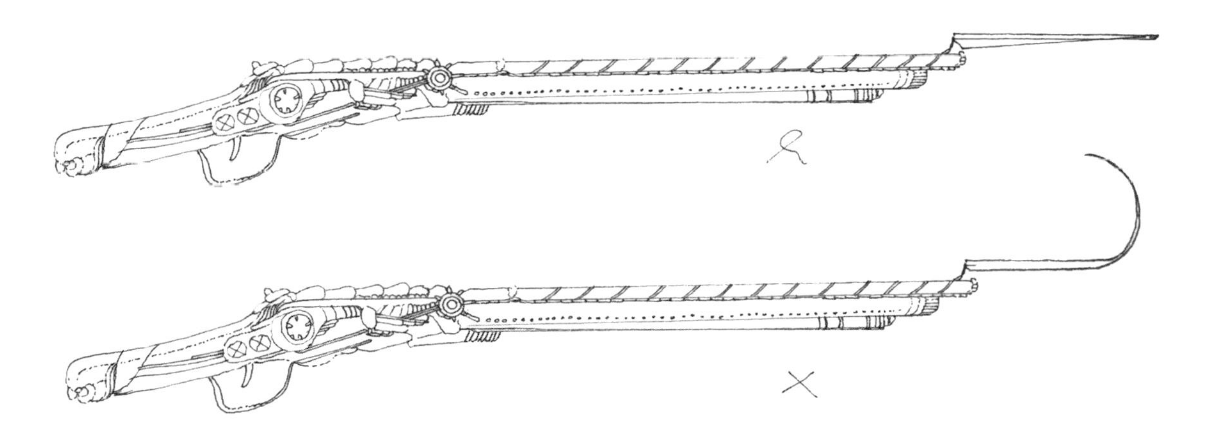

Half-George shook his head. "I suddenly found myself in front of the Castle Killer."

You might as well try to keep bread from rising. Half-George was almost talking to himself, in a dreamy and feverish voice.

"It was a huge cannon, Tortot. The barrel was as wide as two men and the cannonballs were the size of boulders! Two Ottovarians were lighting the fuse. I was about to turn and run, but then I noticed that a third Ottovarian was approaching from behind. He went for my legs with his scimitar. There was nowhere I could go."

"You could have jumped aside, couldn't you?"

"Impossible," said Half-George. "To my left and to my right, there were deep trenches with sharp spikes. If I'd jumped up to avoid the Ottovarian with the

scimitar, my head would have been directly in front of the barrel of the Castle Killer, which was about to fire. So all I could do was stand there and then…"

Half-George cast his eyes down, with a look of dismay.

"I had boots made of chamois leather," he said. "With red tassels. When I'd cleaned them, they gleamed like a fresh cowpat. They belonged to one of my brothers, no, they belonged to an officer first, he'd won them playing dice—my brother, I mean—then he gave them to me, and he said: 'You'll grow into them.' Have I already told you this?"

His lip trembled.

Luckily for Tortot, the camp engineer chose that exact moment to unblock a cannon. That involved stuffing twenty chickens and ten gallons of oil into the barrel. It produced such a blast that Tortot's tent billowed up like a lady's

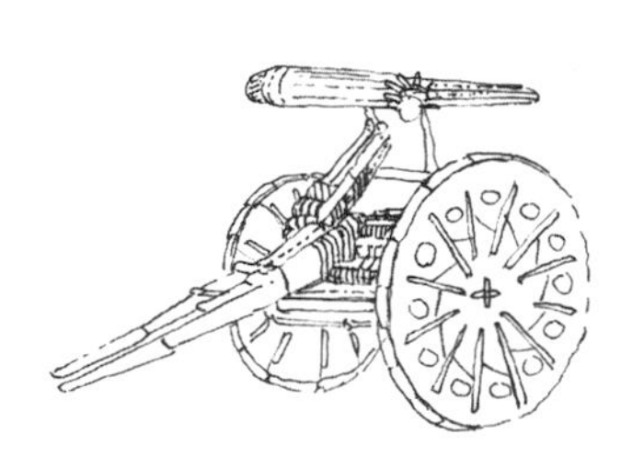
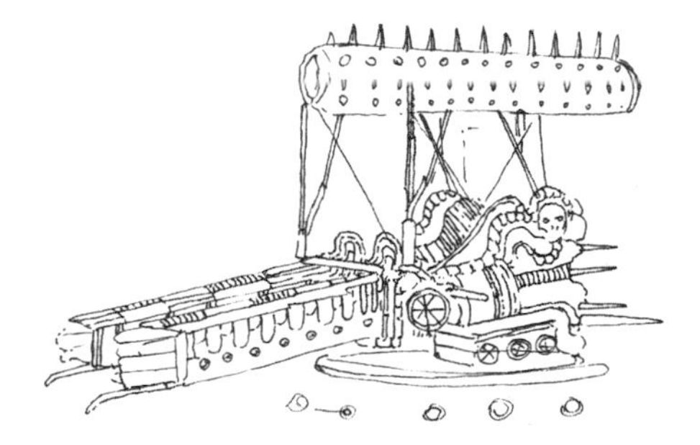
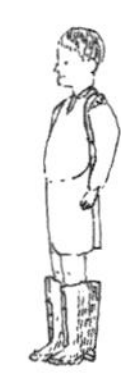

dress in the wind, and twenty freshly launched chickens came rolling in like cackling snowballs, accompanied by a rain of straw and twigs.

Half-George dived to the bottom of his barrel and, to the field cook's relief, he did not show his face for the rest of the day.

Towards the end of the morning, fresh food supplies arrived, escorted by the cavalry.

The insults and curses of the sutlers, the travelling market women, could be heard from afar, as they all tried to be the first to reach the camp with their overloaded carts and donkeys, so that they could pick the best spot to sell their wares.

More than once, a hussar had to risk his own life by stepping in to separate the fighting sutlers.

One of these women had an enormous Ottovarian halberd lying across her cart. This monstrous weapon was one and a half times her size, and she looked like she knew how to use it.

As the women settled in, the camp was engulfed by a wave of vanity. Hussars and artillerymen rubbed lard into their hair and moustaches, polished their buttons and boots and dusted down their coats. A few even washed their faces. This all caused trouble with the ladies of pleasure, who believed their business was threatened and marched off to the makeshift market, their skirts hitched up so high that you could see their bony white knees.

So the colonel, who had witnessed the arrival of the sutlers plenty of times before, imposed a strict rule that their stalls should be set up in a remote corner of the camp. This did not stop the ladies of pleasure throwing stones and mud, though, and uttering curses that, in their creativity and lyricism, were a match for the verses of the greatest poets in the land.

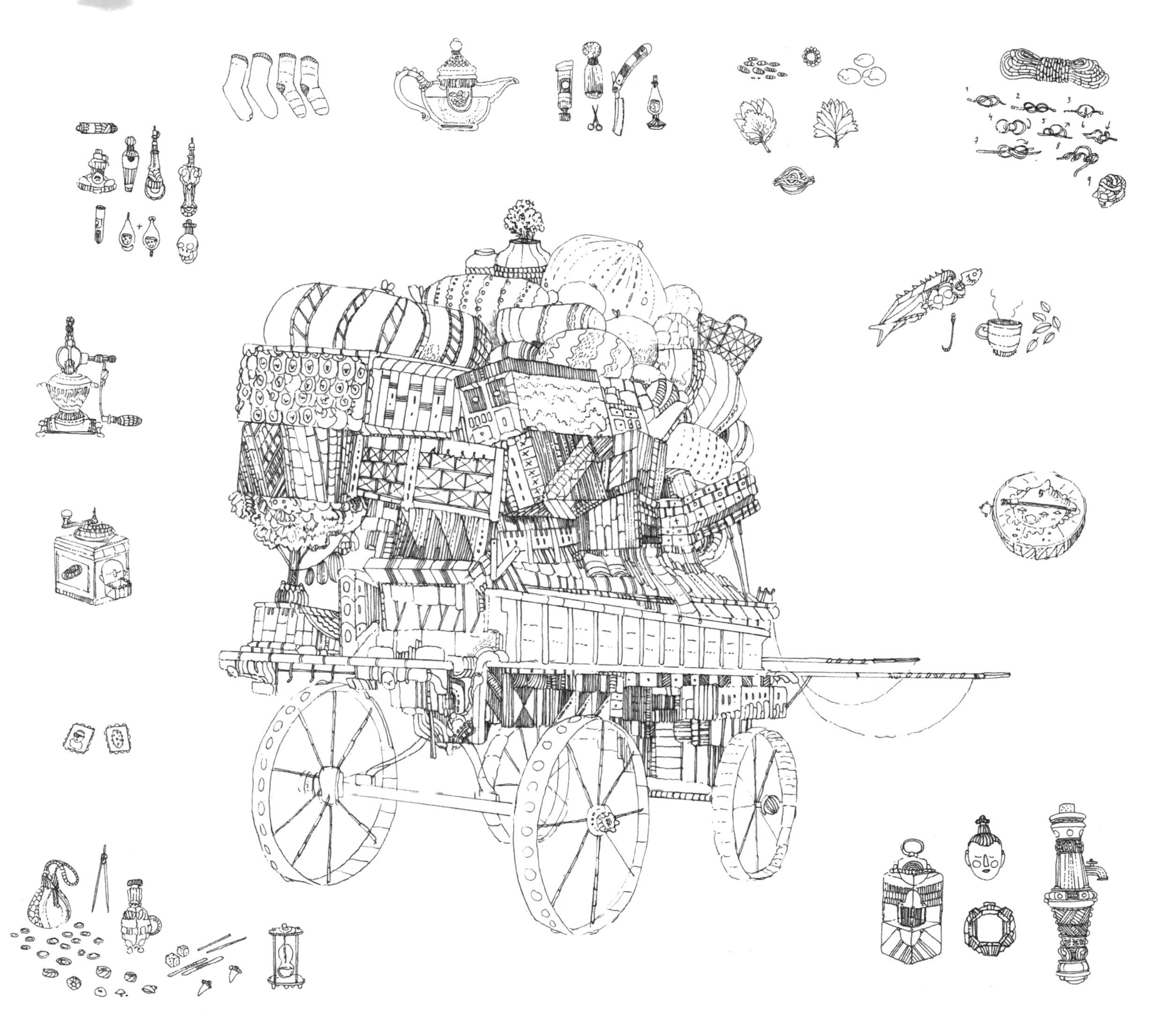

CHAPTER 8

A mother's fate

"Efarim, François! Hurry up! Gerard, Itrahim, Jumeaux! No, put that stick down. Leave the rooster alone. The poor creature's already upset enough. And stop arguing, whatever will your big brothers think? Such an important day, when everyone will see them. Do you want them to hear that their brothers are acting like babies?"

Mother is wearing her tartelette, a hat in the shape of an onion tart. Inside her wicker basket she has three little flasks, each filled with her Eternal Soup, for Bertrand, Clément and Dieudonné. When she gets to the market square and sees her eldest boys there, she straightens their army coats for them. She gives Dieudonné's beret a good beating, as it is already covered with dust because he has been fighting, and she jokes with the baker's wife. She laughs as if she does not have a worry in the world. Tortot, who is clinging to her in the crowd, knows better. She was furious when Clément said they were joining the army. "Didn't I spend the best years of my life raising you?" she screamed. "Haven't I kept food from my own mouth so you wouldn't go hungry? Haven't you noticed how thin I've become? Even though your own father, bless his runaway soul, once fell for the girl with the plumpest thighs and the chubbiest rosy-red cheeks! And now all my hard work will have been for nothing, because my sons have volunteered to be ground up by the imperial mincing machine!"

Bertrand
Age 2

It had not helped. And neither had running straight to the town hall and shouting that her sons were at least a year too young for the war. The army was short of men. Recruiters were handing out military coats. If the hem did not touch the ground, you were old enough.

That evening, Bertrand took their father's shaving mirror from its silk pouch. The three brothers held up the mirror in front of one another's faces; it was well worn. The speckled reflection made them look older, more worldly-wise. Even their voices sounded different. The other brothers gazed at them enviously. Tortot was the only one who did not join in. He watched his mother crying silent tears into the Eternal Soup.

Bertrand
Age 5

Bertrand
Age 11

Bertrand
Age 15

Tortot

CHAPTER 9

In which Tortot has to listen to the most dreadful nonsense and is blackmailed to boot

Tortot was woken by voices. No, not voices. Just one voice. By the weak light of the oil lamp, Half-George was tossing and turning in his barrel. His sweaty forehead gleamed like glass.

"Help! HELP!"

Outside, it was quiet. Even the most dedicated night owls, the sleep-shy hussars, were all flaked out. Even a hedgehog scuttling about would be easily heard on such a quiet windless night, let alone a terrified, screaming boy. Tortot shot up and stumbled across the stone-cold ground to Half-George. "Wake up, you halfwit. Wake up."

Half-George's eyes were open, but they stared blindly ahead.

"They're after me!"

"You're having a nightmare, ssh!"

"Go away! Go away!!"

Tortot took two chili peppers, snipped off the tips, put them in the boy's ears and squeezed. Half-George blinked, shuddered and then gave Tortot a puzzled look.

"You were having a nightmare."

The boy's hair was soaked. Tortot felt his forehead. It was hot. Half-George shook off his hand. "A nightmare?"

"You were dreaming that soldiers were looking for you. Give me that tablecloth. It's soaked through." Irritably, he tugged

at the tablecloth. "How many times have I told you to have a spoonful of sugar before you go to bed? Sweet mouth, sweet dreams. You see what happens when you don't? Now the army's not just outside, but inside you too."

"The army?" Half-George shook his head. The confusion was gone from his eyes. "No, it was my legs."

"What?"

"It wasn't soldiers who were after me. It was my legs."

"Give me that tablecloth. I wouldn't be surprised if you've gone and peed inside your barrel too."

But Half-George clung on to the tablecloth like a drowning man and refused to hand it over until he had told Tortot his whole dream.

"It was war, Tortot. The biggest and most terrible war there had ever been. We were supposed to go and fight, my brothers and me, but we hid. There was a giant tree in the middle of the battlefield. Its branches stretched up into the sky and beyond. Without legs, I couldn't climb, so one brother picked me up, and another carried me, and we went higher and higher. All the way past where the squirrels climb, past where the lark flies, even past where the clouds float. We could see out over all the world. There was war everywhere, but we were safe at the top of the tree."

Tortot handed him a bowl of Eternal Soup. "Here."

Half-George's expression darkened. "Until we saw them coming."

"The soldiers?"

Half-George took a mouthful and began to cough. It was impressive how powerfully that small, frail body could shake.

"My *legs*, Tortot. My legs were coming. Cannons spewed fire, horses galloped the ground to mud, soldiers waved their bayonets around, stabbing left and right, but my legs walked straight through it all. Heading for the tree. They knew where I was. My brothers and I hid around the other side, but my legs just kept following us. In the officer's chamois-leather boots with the tassels. They were shining more than ever before. And no matter what we did, my legs were always standing right beneath us. They were going to betray me and my brothers."

"What nonsense! Why would your own legs want to betray you?"

"Because they were missing me."

"They *what*?"

Half-George nodded. "They were missing me so much that they couldn't stay away. They wanted to, but they just couldn't. And my brothers and I saw soldiers coming from every direction. A group of hussars were hauling the Castle Killer behind them. They headed for the tree, where my legs were waiting for me, and without saying a word, they aimed the Castle Killer, their bayonets and..."

An owl swooped low over the tent with an eerie cry. Tortot suddenly felt just how cold his feet were, like two stones. For a moment, it was as if they were no longer part of him. As if they might walk away from him at any minute, just like Half-George's legs.

The boy looked at Tortot, his face grey with fear. "What if they find me, Tortot?"

"Your legs?"

Half-George shook his head. "The *soldiers*. What if they find me here and what if..."

Tortot shrugged. "'What if' is in the graveyard. Next to 'Maybe' and 'Imagine'."

"But what if..."

"They won't find you."

"Do you promise?"

"What?"

"That they won't find me."

Half-George laid his hand, a scrap of skin and bone, on Tortot's arm.

"Go to sleep," said Tortot.

"Will you make sure they don't find me?"

"Hush now."

Suddenly, the look in Half-George's eyes was strangely sharp and clear. Tortot tried to pull his arm away, but it was like magic. He could not make it move.

"Do you promise?"

Tortot jerked away, but he could still feel Half-George's hand, like a burn. "Stop it. My promises are no good to you. Ask anyone I've ever promised anything to. If they're still alive, that is. Most of them are dead."

"That's their own fault," said Half-George.

"Sorry?"

"They should have believed you."

There were lights in Half-George's eyes. Two seemingly weak lights, like candle flames in a draught, which flicker and yet never go out.

"I'd believe it if you promised me something, Tortot."

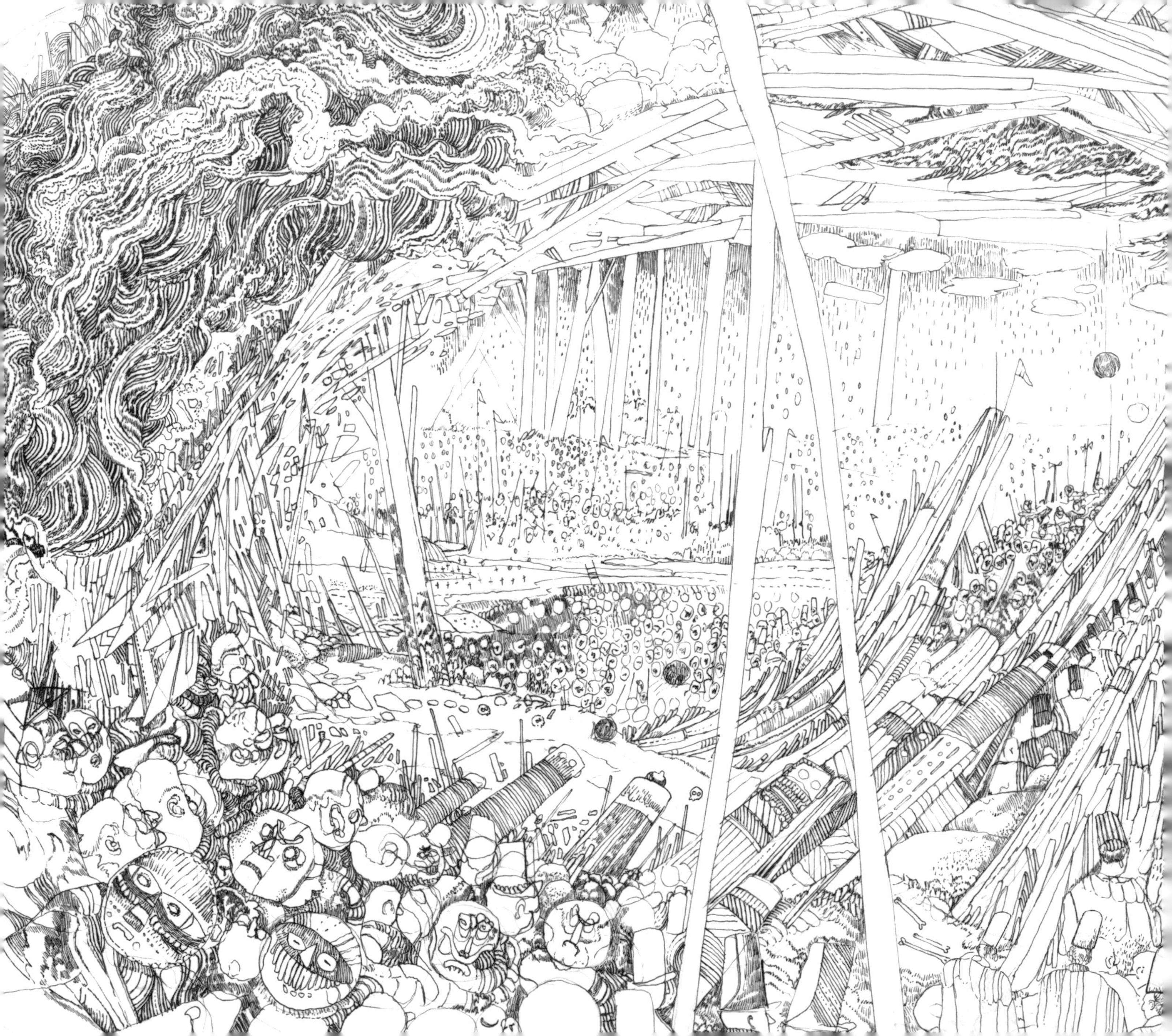

"But I won't do that."

"I could rest easy."

"I'm not promising you anything, Half-George."

"I think I'd even be able to sleep."

"Hey, halfwit, are you deaf or something? What did I just say? I'm not promising you anything, Half-George, not even a grain of salt."

Half-George yawned and stretched. "Do you think it's a full moon, Tortot? It feels like it. Fullmoonish. Is that even a word, fullmoonish?"

"Did you hear what I said?"

"When there's a full moon, you can sometimes hear the angels singing." Half-George yawned again and started wrapping himself up in his tablecloth. "You have to listen carefully, though, if you want to hear it."

"I didn't promise you anything."

"Goodnight, Tortot."

"Half-George..."

"Sleep tight."

"I DIDN'T PROMISE YOU ANYTHING!"

"Hush now. Do you want half the army to hear?"

"You're not safe with me! Hey, bag of bones! Did you hear what I said? Are you listening?"

But Half-George had already fallen asleep. His face soft and relaxed, without even a single furrow, like the face of a dead man.

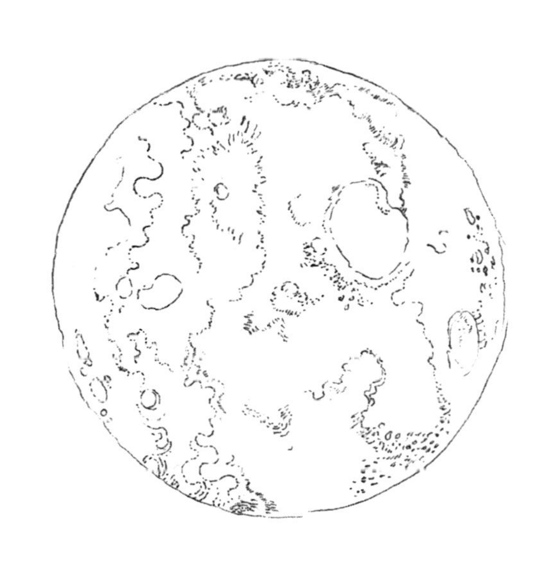

CHAPTER 10

In which the poor field cook is forced to be something he is not

"My feet hurt."

"You don't even have feet anymore."

"I know, but my feet don't seem to care about that."

It was November and a useless day for battles. Snow had fallen, followed by a cruel and freezing rain. The ground had become so slippery that three of the Imperial Emperors' horses had broken their legs and half of an enemy patrol had tumbled into a ravine. Both sides had decided, for financial reasons, to continue the war after the thaw.

The camp was full of sulking, shivering soldiers who were bored to death. Tortot and Half-George could only speak in whispers. Fresh horsemeat was simmering on the fire. The scent of bay leaves wafted through the tent.

"I'm bored," said Half-George. "Will you tell me a story?"

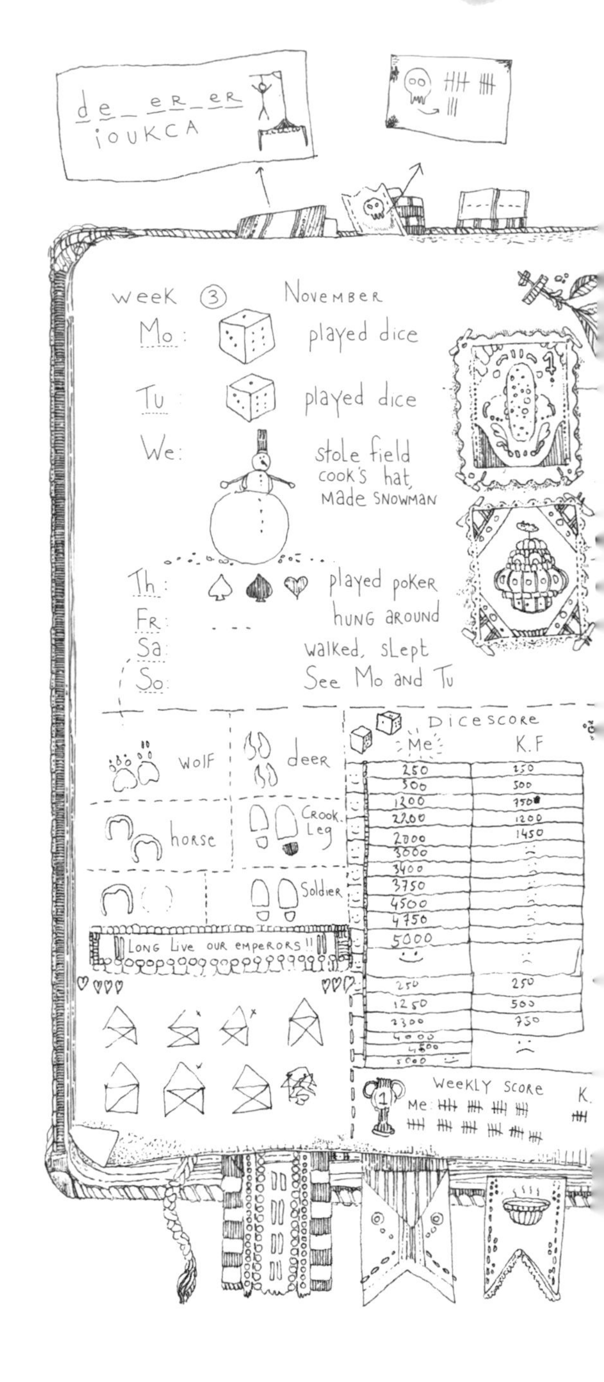

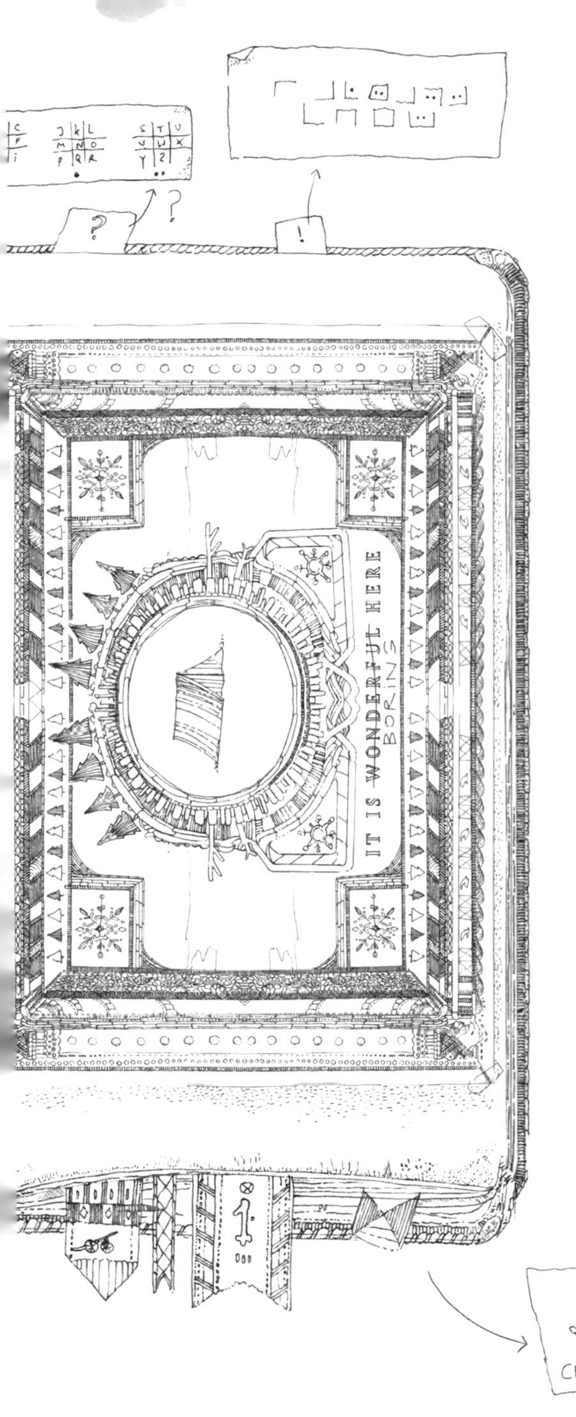

"Do I look like some kind of troubadour?"

Half-George pursed his lips stubbornly. "My brothers know lots and lots of stories."

"Yes, but that's not much good to you now."

"What do you mean?"

"What do you mean by 'What do you mean?'?"

"Why is it no good to me now?"

"Well, you found them, didn't you?"

Half-George shook his head. "No, I forgot the way. I couldn't find the Lounging Lawn. There was just a graveyard."

"But surely you must realize that the..."

"... full of dead people."

"Yes, but your brothers are..."

"And there was no one there. Well, except for a bunch of rooks, but they don't count."

Tortot suddenly felt as tired as a potato in winter soil.

"I'm bored," repeated Half-George.

"Then do whatever you always used to do when you were bored."

"I used to go for a walk."

"Oh."

Half-George began to whine. Quietly enough that the soldiers would not hear, but loud enough to be a threat.

"Stop that."

"A story."

"I don't know any stories."

"It doesn't have to be long."

"I don't know any short stories either."

"Something from the old days."

"The old days are dead."

"A song?"

"When I sing, dead birds fall from the sky."

Half-George's whimpering grew louder.

"Don't go thinking anyone will find you and that you'll get me executed for my stupidity," growled Tortot. "Before a single soldier could enter the tent, I'd have knifed you, skinned you, pickled you and chucked you in with the horsemeat."

Footsteps approached. Tortot could hear how carefully Crookleg was walking. But every time that granite heel hit the icy ground, it was like a pistol going off. Then the sound of a slip and a bump and an angry yell came from outside the tent.

"Cook!"

"Quickly! Into the barrel!" hissed Tortot to Half-George.

"What?" called the sergeant.

"I said: Keep out! There's an oven cooling in here. If it cools down too quickly, the whole place could explode. What's the problem?"

"My father and brother... um... the colonel and the major want to know why there's such a wailing coming from your tent."

"It's all the emotion."

"Emotion?"

"At being able to serve this magnificent army."

"Well, the colonel and the major command you to be emotional more quietly. You're disturbing their game of poker." The shuffling footsteps moved away, but Crookleg had barely gone ten footsteps when Half-George's threatening whimpers from the barrel began again. They rang out like a wet finger running around the rim of a wine glass.

"Fine! Fine!" whispered Tortot. "If I tell you something, halfwit, will you shut your mouth?"

Tortot strode angrily across his kitchen. It was clear that Half-George had lost his mind. And it must be catching. Tortot did not know whether to feel anger or admiration for the boy's pig-headedness.

A story. A story. Where in heaven's name was he going to get a story from?

He stared up at the herbs that were hanging to dry.

Suddenly he knew.

"Pick some sage leaves," said Tortot. "Keep them cool." He paused to think. "No. Wait. Pick sage leaves from a field. A field in the morning. A dewy field in the morning in June. Yes. Carefully twist the stems clockwise and..."

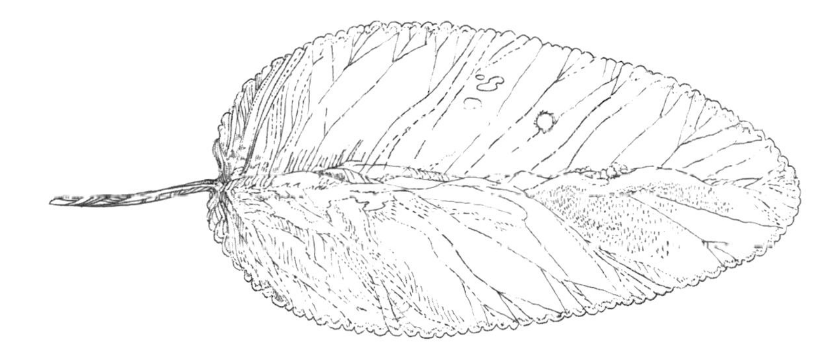

"Tortot?"

"What?"

"I like it already."

"Shut up." Tortot took a deep breath. "Wrap the sage leaves in a damp cloth and um... keep them cool. Then take two partridges. Preferably, young partridges. Young partridges who have lived a fine life. Let the partridges scratch around for a while by the house. And doze in the shade of an old oak tree. Feed them fermenting juniper berries. Let them, um... fall asleep on your lap. Stroke their little heads until they doze off. Tickle them gently. Just at the back of their necks. They like that. No, they love that. It's something they really enjoy."

Isn't it strange what words can do? The way you can turn them into a day in June? Or a crooked house with a crooked garden? Or everything all at once?

"Twist the partridges' necks with just one quick movement. Pluck their feathers. Cradle them in garlic and pepper and the sage leaves. Gently lull them on the fire. Sprinkle them with Chardonnay, just a dash. Let them simmer for a long time."

From the barrel came soft, regular breathing. Tortot looked around in a daze. It was a moment before he saw canvas again instead of crooked walls. And before the June sunshine gave way to the drumming of yet more freezing rain.

CHAPTER 11

In which the brave Tortot creates the Imperial Law regarding Contamination

One morning, just after the watery winter sun had risen, there was a sound of shouting and cursing. Soldiers' boots clattered past the field kitchen. Tortot poked his head out of the tent just in time to see a man being dragged roughly through the snow. A man? It was more like a bag of bones.

Tortot soon found out what had happened. The poor soul had hidden in one of the birch groves close to the camp and kept himself alive for weeks by eating birch bark and drinking snow water. But the heady scents of Tortot's cooking had made him less cautious. He had been found, half-crazed with hunger, beside the snow-covered rubbish dump at the edge of the camp, sucking the marrow from a frozen chicken bone.

No one knew exactly which army he was from. The soldier's jacket was from the East Sevelian army, but the silk knickerbockers with the bows and frills were clearly Avançan. Not to mention the helmet with the crescent moon on it and the oriental inscription.

There was no way to ask him now. Out of sheer boredom, a few of the soldiers had beheaded the man. Then the soldiers were themselves executed, but that had not brought peace back to the camp. Far from it.

Crookleg hobbled into the field kitchen, followed by a handful of soldiers. "Inspection! Every tent is to be searched for enemy elem..."

He fell silent and stared at the field cook, who was calmly stirring a pot of soup.

"Adjutant Nilliewasser!" said Tortot. "How nice of you to come and visit me."

"That's *Sergeant* Nilliewasser," Crookleg reluctantly corrected him. "As you well know."

"Still?" said Tortot, looking downright amazed. "Does that mean you've been passed over? Again?"

"Be quiet."

"But wasn't the only one who was eligible to become adjutant—other than you—that fool..."

"Silence."

"... with the squint..."

"Silence, I said!"

"... you know, the one who almost shot off his own foot the other day?"

Crookleg brought his face very close to Tortot's. A muscle beside his right eye was twitching. Spittle frothed at the corners of his mouth like blobs of whisked egg white. "Listen, you grubby, horrible little cook, everyone else might lose their mind when you cook, but not me. I'd be careful if I were you. Very careful indeed."

Crookleg ordered the soldiers to search the tent thoroughly. Tortot let them do their work. He ignored it when they dug around in his herb cabinet with their filthy paws, and he blew a lock of hair out of his face when the soldiers made unsightly scratches on his oven with their bayonets. But when they came to the barrel of gherkins, he spoke up.

"Article 212."

"What?"

"You do know Article 212, don't you? The Imperial Law regarding Contamination? The Imperial Gherkin Barrel may not be opened for any reason other than Imperial consumption! Surely you must be aware of Article 212!"

The sergeant turned to his soldiers. "Open that barrel."

Tortot whistled appreciatively. "Very clever," he said. "And there's the proof."

You could see Crookleg was determined not to say any more than was necessary, and definitely not to ask the question that Tortot was dangling in front of his nose like a carrot. But his curiosity got the better of him.

"The proof of what?"

"How unfair it is that you've never been promoted."

Crookleg stared at him suspiciously.

"Of course, the death penalty only applies to whoever opens the barrel," Tortot added casually.

The soldiers jumped and pulled their hands away.

And as the sergeant went to open the barrel himself, Tortot added: "I don't think your brother will be too happy about this. Not to mention your father. He's the one who's in charge of promotions, isn't he?"

Crookleg limped back outside as fast as he could.

Tortot knew he had taken a big gamble. Even an idiot like Crookleg would find out sooner or later that the "Imperial Law regarding Contamination" did not exist.

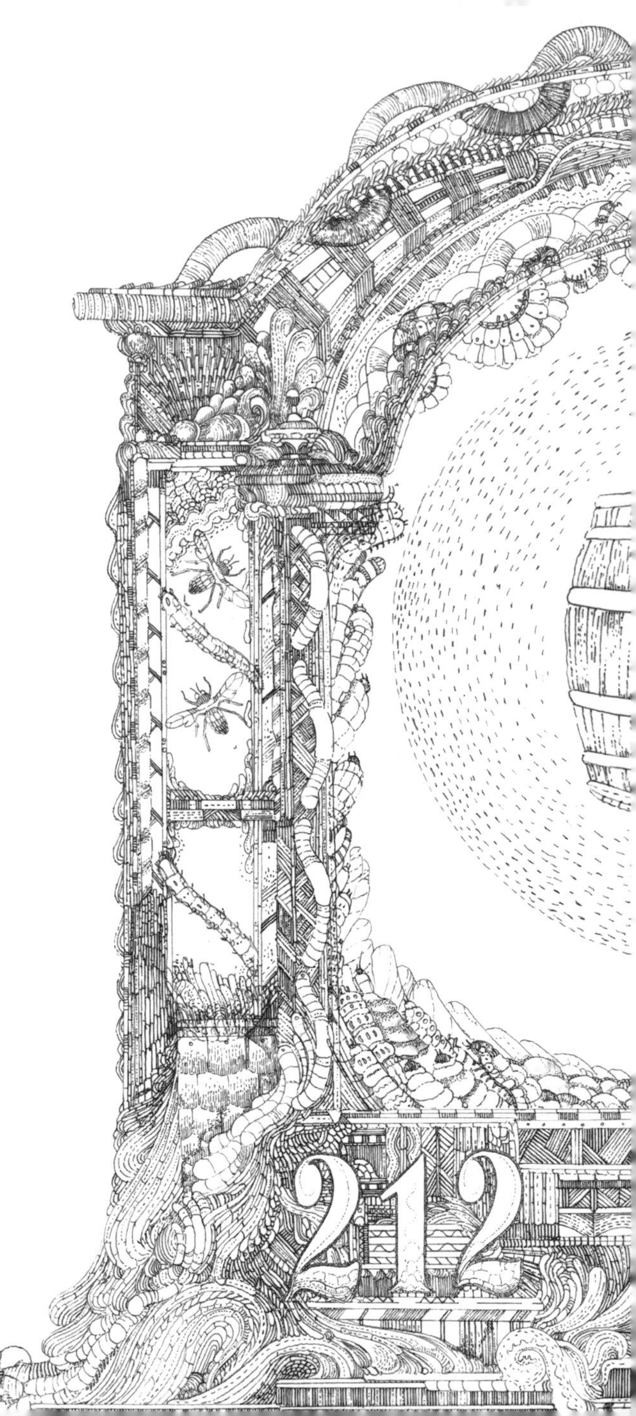

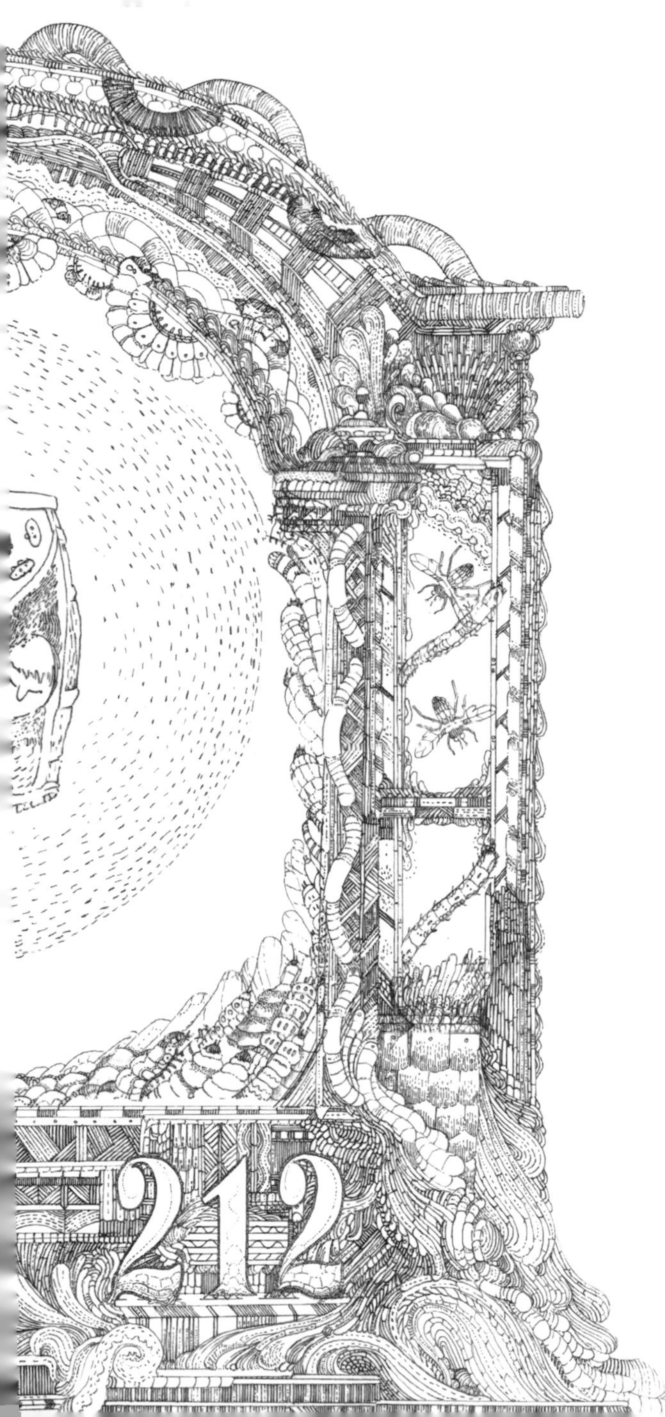

It took the field cook almost three hours to make a removable rim around the top of the barrel, consisting of a wooden ring, which he sealed with an oiled pig's bladder, so that the compartment could be filled with vinegar. From then on, anyone who did not know any better would take off the lid and think they were looking at a barrel that was filled to the brim.

Just when every corner of the camp had been searched and peace was starting to return, the sutlers came back. This time they arrived with a great deal less commotion than before. The group had thinned out. In fact, there were only five left—and two of them turned out to be working for the sutler with the Ottovarian halberd. It was anyone's guess why the group had shrunk like that. It seemed unlikely that anyone would have dared to attack that bunch of wild furies. Was it illness? Had the other sutlers chosen a different, more lucrative camp to supply? Had they been bought off by the Ottovarian sutler? Had she threatened them with her halberd?

The goods sold by the Ottovarian and her companions were by far the best.

They sold not only fresh vegetables and chickens and partridges tied to sticks, but also tobacco and brandy. They tapped beer from small oak barrels. Much of their wares consisted of ointments for syphilis, concoctions for scurvy and a potion for "nights of strength". The most popular items were her wishing strips made from the rice paper used for communion wafers. The Ottovarian swore that these pieces of edible paper came from the Holy of Holies in Rome, and for a fee she would use cherry juice to write her customers' hearts' desires on a strip. Once it was eaten, the wish would come true within a month.

As proof, she displayed thank-you letters from soldiers who had won over the most beautiful girl in the village, or seen their mother recover from consumption, or found a fortune at the bottom of their vegetable garden, wrapped inside the leaves of a cabbage. No one seemed concerned that the letters were all in the same handwriting, which was suspiciously like the handwriting of the Ottovarian herself.

Apart from writing these wishes, the Ottovarian left most of the work to her two companions. She sat there, wide-legged in her harem pants, smoking sweet cigarettes and playing solitaire, with the Ottovarian halberd leaning against a tree behind her. The eight-foot-long

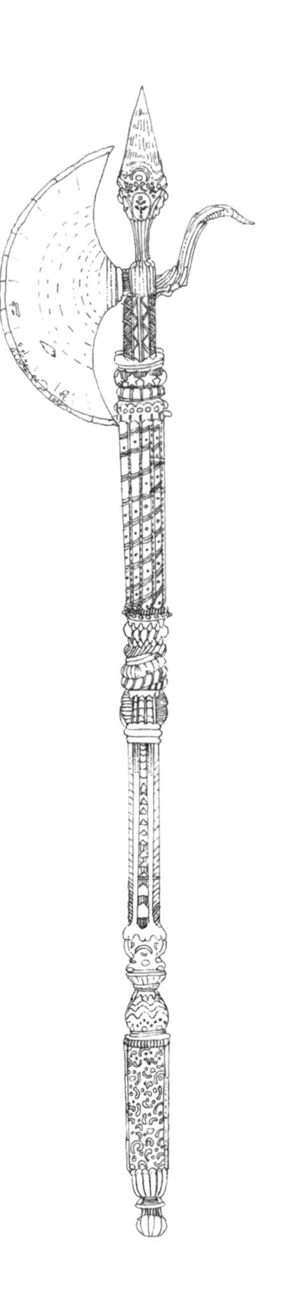

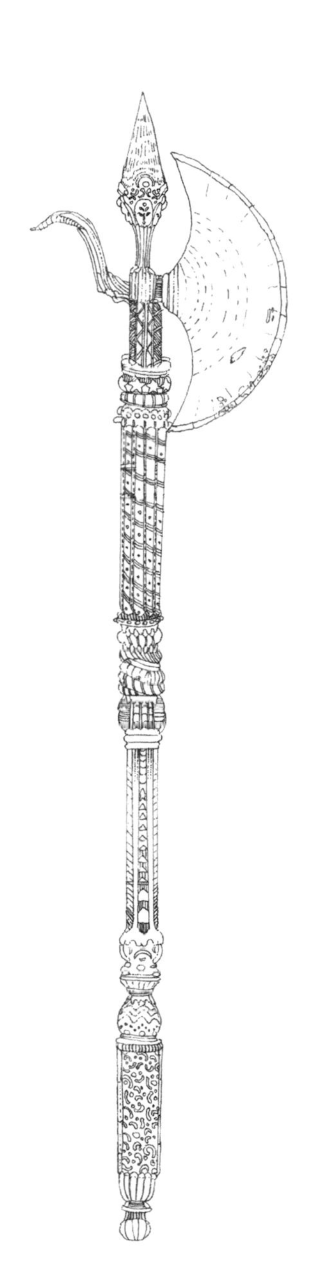

weapon, with its razor-sharp point and curving blade, ensured that the ladies of pleasure, who came flocking, still uttering the most poetic curses and insults, did not get any foolish ideas in their heads.

No one knew how the sutler had got her hands on the halberd. Some said that with her sharp bargaining skills she could even persuade God to sell his angels, so in all likelihood she had haggled some kind of deal for the weapon. Others whispered that she was the former mistress of an Ottovarian officer—no, that she was Ottovarian herself. She was, after all, as acrobatic and flamboyant as a lady from the harem. The sutler was wily enough to feed this stream of rumours; nothing is better for business than unsatisfied curiosity, she always said, and so she did her calculations in Ottovarian.

"See anything to your liking, field cook?"

Tortot pulled a critical expression and, with studied indifference, he fondled the cauliflowers, carrots, lettuces and radishes.

The sutler watched with the same studied indifference. Her eyes were rimmed with kohl. A scar ran from beneath her eye past her nose to just above her top lip. She had lost the thumb on her left hand.

They negotiated for a long time. Not that it mattered to Tortot, as the supplies were paid for by the quartermaster, a complete scatterbrain, but he liked the shrewd, sharp game that the sutler played. Although her face, in spite of the scar, was almost ageless, this was clearly not her first war.

"Do you have a name?" asked Tortot, after the deal was sealed. It just popped out, he had no idea why he had asked, and he instantly felt embarrassed.

For a moment it looked as if she would spit at his feet.

"Couraz."

"Tortot," said Tortot, feeling more and more ridiculous.

"As if I didn't know that already."

That night, the moon had fallen from the sky. And somewhere in the pitch-dark night, Half-George must have sneaked out of his barrel and into Tortot's bed. He lay opposite the field cook, with his head at the foot of the camp bed. Half-George's breath was thin and reedy.

For a moment, Tortot thought about sending him packing, but the lad would likely just come creeping back as soon as Tortot went back to sleep. It would be better simply to ignore him.

Just before sunrise, there was a scratching sound from the pots and pans. A pot rolled over. Tortot felt Half-George freeze and then shoot upright.

An ice-cold blast of wind gusted under the warm covers. Tortot pulled the covers straight. "It was just a mouse or a rat, boy. Lie down. I don't want to catch another cold."

Half-George lay back down. A ridiculously small bump for a boy of twelve.

"Tortot?"

"What?"

"Weren't you scared when the soldiers searched your tent?"

"I'm never scared."

"Really?"

"Never."

"What about sad?"

"No. Never. And do you want to know why?"

"Yes."

"Because I have the heart of a fish. Have you ever seen a fish crying? And now shut up and go to sleep."

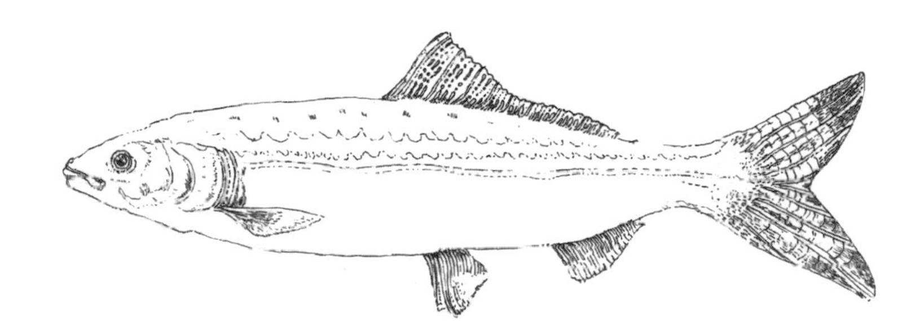

CHAPTER 12

In which the Son Collector looks for a son and catches a mother

One day a coach crashed into the crooked village's water pump at full speed.

It was not the first time this had happened. Scattered around, here and there, lay the remains of previous accidents: a wheel without spokes, a coachman's broken whip and the fleshless skull of a horse.

The reason for all these accidents was the road that led from the mountains to the valley where the village lay. Halfway along that road stood an enormous obelisk. And, behind that obelisk, the road took a turn before a terrifying plunge into the village. But because the obelisk was so large, only part of the slope could be seen.

Admittedly, there was a wooden board beside the stone saying "Danger! Steep road!", but strangers to the area paid no attention. At the time, the fashion among bandits was to place such signs at blind spots along the road and then to attack travellers as soon as they slowed down. Not even a later sign that was added—"This is not a trick!"—could stop travellers from urging their horses to go faster just before the bend. Because bandits also put up such signs when the first sign had ceased to have an effect.

That was how the Son Collector's visit to the crooked village began: with his coach smashed to pieces and the shaft broken in two. The horse had broken free of its harness. The coachman was still up front, unconscious.

Now, the Son Collector had seen a thing or two. Throughout his thankless career, he had managed to avoid being tarred and feathered, just as he had been spared being pelted with eggs, hanged on the spot or lynched. This was mainly due to the papal signet ring that he wore, as a sign of divine protection.

And if that did not help, then the hundred soldiers who followed him were sufficient.

In the last alley at the end of the village was a house that, if possible, was even more crooked than all the other houses. He was received in the darkest room.

"Name?"

"Jumeaux."

"Born in this place?"

"Indeed."

"Age?"

"Fifteen."

The boy was wrapped in a cloak and hood. When the lad took the goose-feather quill to place a cross by his name, the Son Collector saw that he had remarkably small and old hands for a boy of his age. There was also a white circle around his ring finger. The Son Collector sighed and stopped the hand before it could sign.

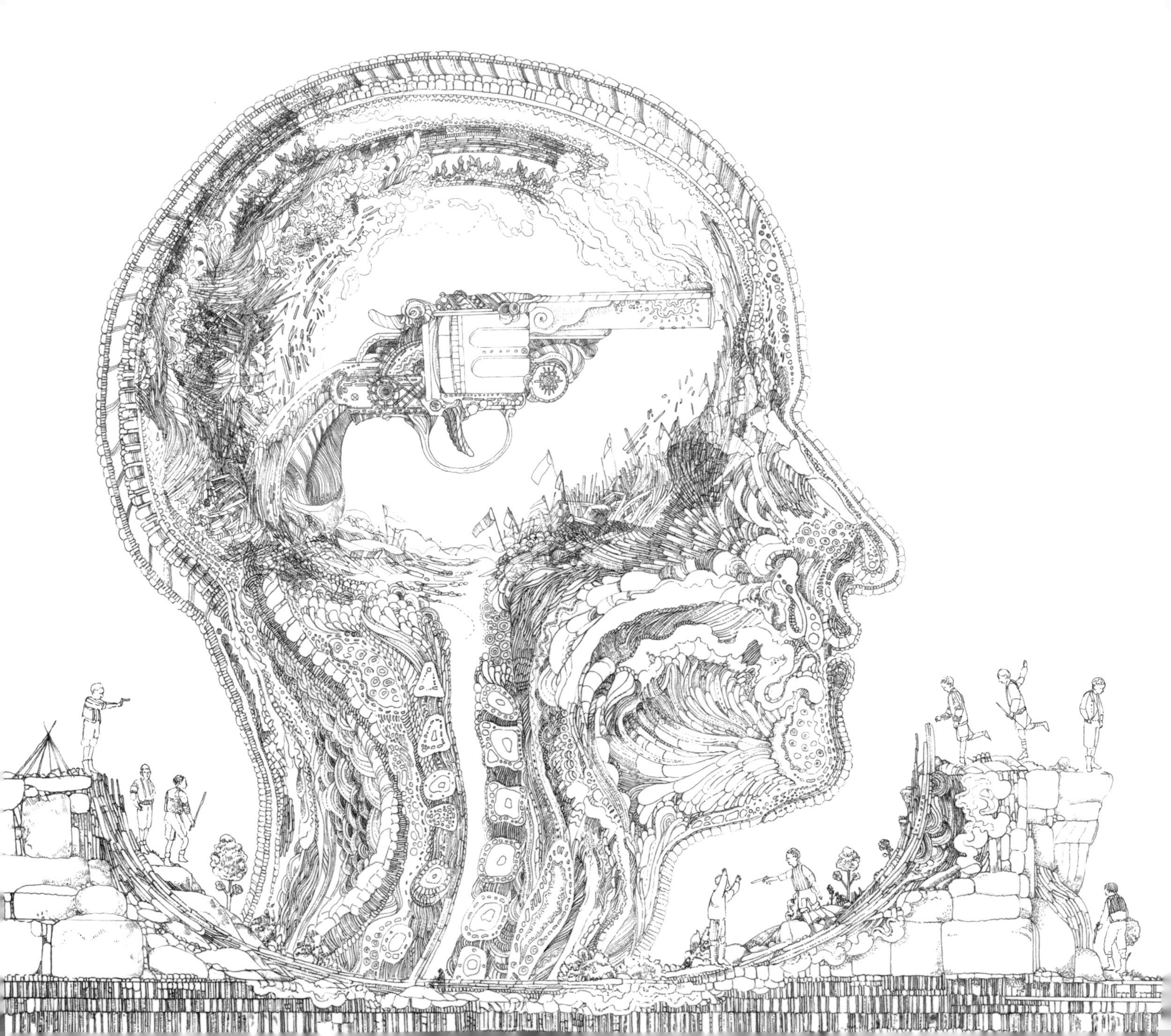

"Madam, please. There is no point," he said softly.

The hand tried to press down on the paper with force, to make the cross. The Son Collector shook his head. He had no idea who had started the story that only the person who signed had to go to war. But it was a rumour that refused to die, and one that was particularly popular with mothers who were trying to keep their sons from the battlefield.

This mother was younger and healthier than he had thought, or at least her anger was certainly robust. When the soldiers searched the house and found her son (locked up in the chicken shed) and put an army coat on him that just failed to reach the ground, she boiled over like hot soup.

"Everyone can see that coat's been taken up!" she cried. She lifted the hem of the coat, before the soldiers could stop her. "Look! It's been made shorter and shorter, war after war. If you go on like this, you'll soon be sending infants to war!"

"Mum," the boy said with a scowl. "I want to go."

She boxed him about the ears. And then again. And then she rained down blows on him. The boy stood there as if she were a hailstorm, not resisting, his shoulders tight with shame.

"Of course you want to go!" she yelled. "Every boy's head is full of war."

And she shouted at the Son Collector that she had spent the best years of her life raising her sons, yes, sir. And kept food from her own mouth so that they would not go hungry. And now all that hard mothering work was going to be wiped out by a bunch of idiots who were too big for their boots?!

The Son Collector could have had her arrested for insulting the authorities, but the prisons were already overcrowded. And mothers were the biggest troublemakers of all.

When the boy picked up the quill to sign, it took two soldiers hold her back, but as the scratching on the paper stopped, all the anger seemed to flow out of her. She looked at the Son Collector. Her cheeks were still fiery-red, but her eyes were calm.

"May I ask you something?"

He wanted to ignore her. Or to snarl at her that mothers should know their place. But those eyes…

"What do you think mothers are made of?"

"Sorry?"

"What do you think mothers are made of?" she repeated.

"Um…"

"Flesh, blood, bones?"

"Um… That seems like… uh… yes?"

She shook her head. "Mothers are made of sons. And when those sons are no longer there, they might as well not be there either."

"Console yourself," said the Son Collector. He meant to say it sternly, but that, too, was a failure. He looked at the little boy who was clinging to her and gazing up at him with wide eyes. "The army can never ask for more than eight sons. At least you have one left. He'll never have to go to war."

Her fury returned in a crashing wave.

"One left!" she screeched after him. "One left out of nine! That's supposed to be a consolation? A consolation?! That?!"

8
4
3
1
7
5
2
6

CHAPTER 13

In which the ingenious Tortot turns two soldiers into one

Half-George stared listlessly at his bowl of Eternal Soup.

"Eat," said Tortot.

"Huh, what do you care?"

"What do I care? Nothing at all. Less than nothing, in fact, but I won't have you insulting my dear departed mother."

Half-George dropped his spoon into the bowl with a splash.

"I could always call the soldiers," said Tortot.

"But you won't."

"I wonder what your brothers would say if they saw you like this."

Half-George looked at him defiantly. "My brothers are dead."

"Sorry?"

"Dead."

Tortot walked calmly to his herb cabinet and took out some mustard seed, aniseed and garlic. He put them in his mortar, added sea salt and carefully began crushing the ingredients.

"The Lounging Lawn doesn't even exist," said Half-George.

"Oh?"

"Straight through the camp, left after the birch wood, right at the dead oak and then over the river. That's what you said. And that's where the graveyard is."

Shaking his head, Tortot pointed the pestle at Half-George. "No, you dope. *Right* after the birch wood and *left* at the dead oak. That's what I said."

"No, it isn't."

"If you say so."

"You made it up."

"Whatever you say."

"They're in the graveyard, Tortot, and you know it!"

Half-George's voice sounded hard, but his eyes showed that the dam was about to burst. Tortot pretended not to notice. He crushed and mashed until he had created a shiny green mixture. "So what about all those times I served refreshments on the Lounging Lawn? All those times I cooked spit-roasted chicken? Did I make that up too?"

"Then what does it look like, this Lounging Lawn?"

"What kind of question is that?"

"Go on. Describe it."

"It's a meadow."

"What kind of meadow?"

"A green one."

"Every meadow's green."

"Let me finish, halfwit! The Lounging Lawn is green, yes. But throughout the green there's a golden-purple haze. That's the golden-purple king poppy."

"Never heard of it."

"No, of course you haven't. The golden-purple king poppy is one of the rarest and most delicate flowers in the world. It doesn't normally grow in these parts. But the Lounging Lawn lies in a sheltered dip. The harsh north wind can't blow there. Ever. So the golden-purple king poppy flourishes like a weed."

It was unlikely that Half-George believed him. He was probably just tired of Tortot's nagging. But he ate half of the soup. Soon after that, he fell asleep, exhausted, his cheeks flushed, beads of sweat on his brow.

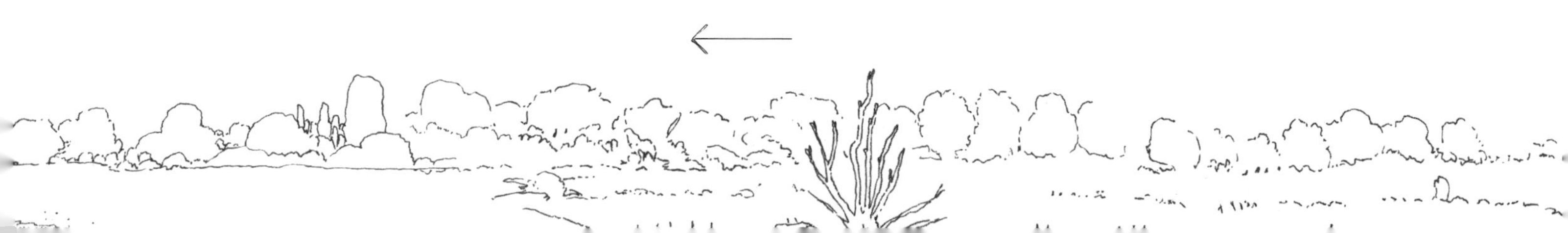

Tortot had known for some time. The boy was ill. He had realized back when he made the fake rim for the gherkin barrel. First he had given the entire barrel a thorough scrub. Once the overpowering smell of vinegar had gone, the scent it had been masking emerged, a sickly, ailing odour. The smell of rot.

Gangrene.

Tortot had seen it before. Soldiers would recover from the amputation of a limb and fight on for days, sometimes weeks, without a hint of pain or difficulty. With enough fighting spirit for ten men. And then, suddenly, they would keel over.

Gangrene.

If you did nothing to treat it, the diseased tissue would turn first red, then green, blue and finally black. But by that point, the patient was unaware of it. By then he was already half-crazed with fever. And no surgeon in the world could save him.

For one moment—one blissful moment—it occurred to Tortot that he would soon be able to bury the lad. And, along

with him, all the worry of recent days. But that moment passed.

He called in a soldier. "I'm looking for a good wine for the officers this evening. You seem like a man with taste. Would you like to help me?"

The soldier, a balding man with a beer belly, nodded eagerly.

Less than an hour later, the man was conked out, with bottles scattered all around him. Tortot dragged the man onto the table and laid him on his back. Half-George was already sleeping (a potion from under the field cook's hat). He carefully picked up the unconscious boy and placed him on his back too. He slid the soldier and Half-George together. Then he put a sheet over them, so that only the soldier's head and Half-George's halved lower section could be seen.

The surgeon was old and as bent as a bow, but all the amputations he had carried out with a saw had given him the arms of a circus strongman.

Tortot first dished up a hearty onion soup for him, then a stew, and finally he served a delicious crème brûlée.

"A friend of yours?" asked the surgeon, dabbing his lips with the linen cloth that Tortot handed him. He pointed at the table the soldier was lying on.

"A very dear friend," said Tortot.

"What's his name?"

Tortot stared at the face of the unknown soldier. "Um... Willem."

With the utmost precision, the surgeon spooned the last bit of crème brûlée from his bowl. A man who can scrape so very precisely, thought Tortot, has to be a good surgeon.

The surgeon pointed at the soldier with his spoon. "So what happened to Umwillem?"

"A little accident in the kitchen."

The physician stretched. With one last wistful glance at the empty plates, he stood up. He ran his tongue around his mouth and smacked his lips. Picked something from between his teeth and looked at it with interest. "Must have been quite some little accident."

"My knife slipped."

"Strange," said the surgeon. He began whistling a tune.

"How do you mean?"

The surgeon stood beside the unconscious man. "The wound seems to have stitched itself up. Not too accurately, it's actually something of a disaster, but still..."

Tortot said nothing.

"But the strangest thing," said the surgeon, "is the remarkable rejuvenation of the tissue."

He stared at the soldier's hairy arm and then at Half-George's smooth skin.

"What's it going to cost?" asked Tortot. "To help my friend, I mean."

The surgeon looked at Tortot with a blank, neutral expression. Then he started whistling. Tortot could not help joining in. When you think that the two men had never whistled together before, it sounded very fine indeed. It began with a march, which turned into a mazurka and ended in a melancholy waltz. When the last note had faded, the surgeon said: "I wouldn't mind some more of that crème brûlée. Let's say once a week. The onion soup was very tasty, but my guts couldn't take it every week. So you can alternate with oxtail soup. And I'd like to swap the stew for some more substantial meat. A joint. Not pork."

"That's all?" asked Tortot, surprised.

The surgeon shrugged. He was so stooped that this almost made him topple forward. "A man you can whistle with is a man you should treasure."

The surgeon cleaned the wound. Now and then a young and boyish groan came from under the sheet, somewhere around the soldier's stomach. Tortot did not worry. The herb he had given Half-George would keep him asleep until the following morning.

Two hours later, the surgeon was finished.

"Is he going to get better?"

The man gave him a vague smile.

"I did what I could, but my resources are limited. The rot has stopped for now. He'll be vulnerable, though, for as long as he stays in the camp. War is no place for the wounded."

4/4
4/4
pppp f mpp
4/4
4/4
3/4
3/4

CHAPTER 14

In which the good and honest Tortot confesses everything and yet does not get arrested

One crisp and freezing morning, Tortot hitched his bespectacled donkey to his cart and loaded the gherkin barrel onto the back. The guards at the exit from the camp stopped him.

"Orders of the Imperial Emperors," Tortot said loudly. "This barrel of gherkins is in need of some fresh air." He leaned forward to the soldiers and said quietly, "Please stop me."

The soldiers looked at each other.

"I like sitting by my fire as much as you do," Tortot explained, as he looked around. "Anything's better than traipsing around the woods for two hours in this cold weather. A barrel isn't a cow. It doesn't need fresh air and exercise." He unobtrusively took out his money bag, which had grown fuller every time Tortot had changed camp.

A look of greed came into the soldiers' eyes.

"And I don't really believe," continued the field cook, "that everyone who stops the barrel will be hanged, drawn and quartered. How many times has that happened in recent years? Once or twice? Well, all right, let's call it three. But more than that? Absolutely not."

The soldiers turned about-face and raised the barrier.

"Come on," begged Tortot. "There are wolves out there the size of bullocks! I've got gout. And anyway, who says I've really got Imperial gherkins in the barrel? I could have hidden a deserter in there!"

The guards themselves pushed Tortot's cart past the felled tree that was serving as a barrier. The bespectacled donkey bucked.

Tortot could not remember how long he had had the donkey. He thought he had bought it at some point between wars three and four, but it could have been seven and eight. The animal was at the market with four pigs and an ox. It had been at the end of the day. Whatever was left by then was cheap, but there was always something wrong with it. The pigs had ear infections and no tails, and the ox was strong enough to pull three ploughs, but it would only walk backwards.

There did not seem to be anything wrong with the donkey though. It was young and tame, which is not the easiest combination to find. Tortot walked with the animal to the local slaughterhouse, where a pig was being slaughtered. A good test for the battlefield. Dreamily, the donkey stared at the blood that was gushing out on the ground. The pig's shrieking did not seem to disturb it in the slightest.

"A bargain!" said the trader.

Of course Tortot knew there was something fishy about this donkey, but the problem could not be insurmountable.

It was only when he fell asleep on the donkey on his way home from the market, and the animal walked first into a ditch and then mistook the river for the road (Tortot only just managed to stop it from walking into the swirling black water) and finally bumped its head really hard into an oak tree that Tortot began to have his suspicions.

"No, not blind," said the surgeon in Tortot's army at the time. "I would say: extremely short-sighted."

As the donkey had barely reacted to the screams of the pig, Tortot thought it likely that it was stone-deaf as well.

He could, of course, have got rid of the creature. A short-sighted, stone-deaf donkey is not much use in a war zone. But it was really strong, willing and so

completely unflappable that, a week later, Tortot bought two lorgnettes and had the saddler sew the lenses into a pair of horse blinkers. That made the little donkey the only beast of burden in the world that could see more with its blinkers on.

The field cook drove the cart along the snowy path through the birch trees. It was freezing-cold and the sunlight was weak, but the song of a solitary blackbird rang out through the woods, determined, unstoppable.

Half-George had lifted the lid half off the barrel. Tortot could almost feel the boy's excitement. Occasionally, he heard him inhale deeply.

The speed of Half-George's recovery from the operation was remarkable. The fever was gone within two days, and his face, although still as pale as a corpse, seemed less thin. The nasty smell of rot coming from the barrel had largely disappeared, but more was needed for a complete recovery, the surgeon had said. Fresh air could do him a lot of good.

"Where are we going?"

"To the river."

When Tortot looked around, he saw Half-George's gratefully gleaming eyes peeping over the edge of the barrel. The cook tutted. "Don't get any big ideas, squib. I need some fresh herbs. And if I'd left you there alone, you can bet your boots that Crookleg would have decided to order another search."

Travel through the area was relatively safe. The land all the way to the river was in the hands of the Imperial Emperors. And even if they bumped into a lost enemy patrol, chances were that it would keep to the ceasefire. No one liked to breathe new life into a war in winter.

"Tortot?"

"What?"

"Are you really never scared or sad?"

"That's right."

"Because you have the heart of a fish."

"Exactly."

"And fish never cry."

"Bingo."

It was quiet for a while. Tortot felt his ears ringing. Usually, silence was to war what water was to the desert. And Half-George must actually like silence, too, deep down, because the lad had not said anything for at least two min—

"Tortot?"

Tortot raised his eyes to the heavens.

"Tortot?"

Just ignore it. Lalala. Pompompom.

"Tortot? Tortot? Tortottortottortot?"

"WHAT IS IT THIS TIME?"

Startled, a couple of wood pigeons flew up into the sky. Something fell out of a tree nearby.

"Where were you born?"

"Somewhere near my mother."

"No. Really."

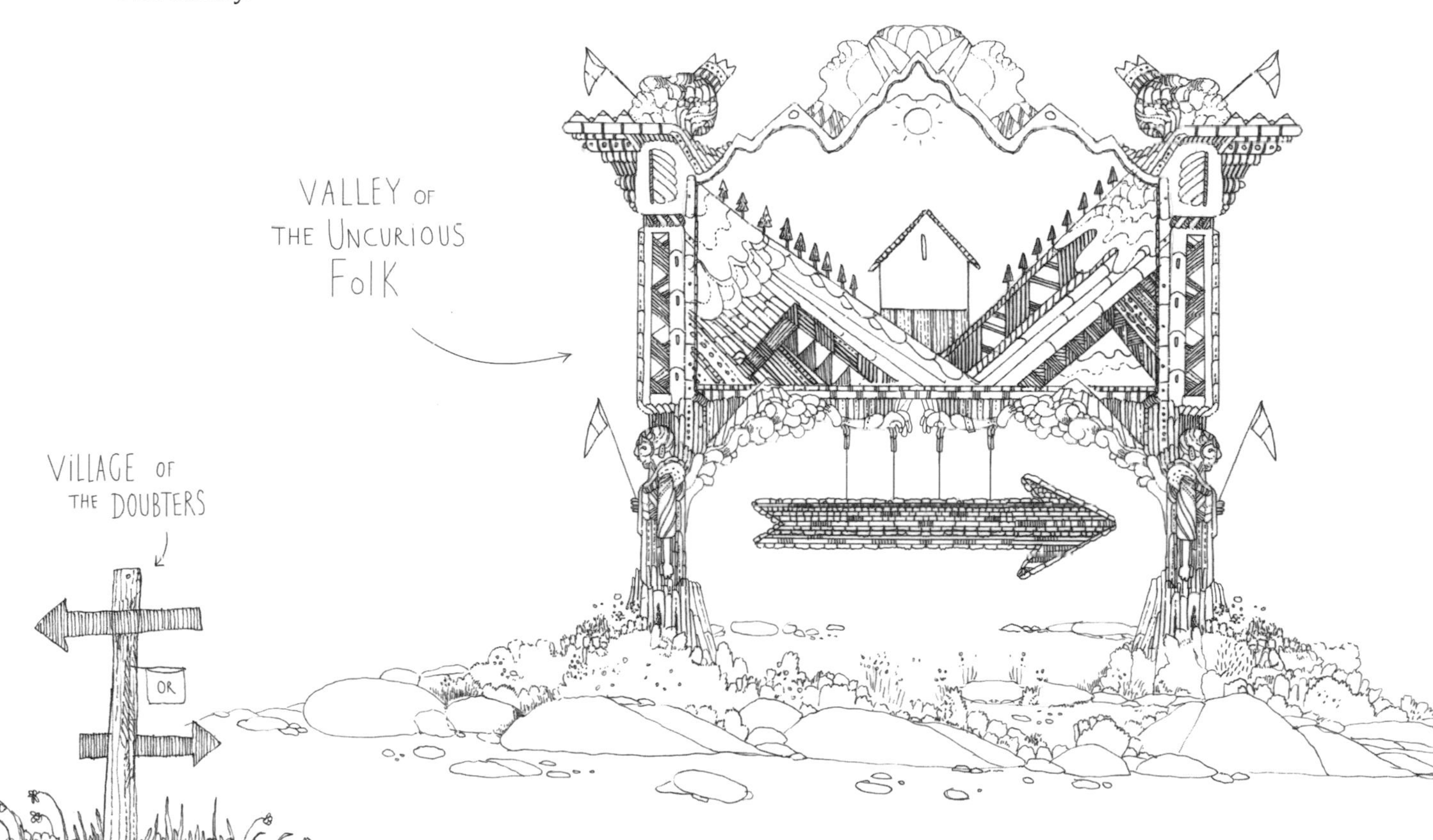

"Somewhere between here and there."

"You can tell me, can't you?"

Tortot gave a very long and very deep sigh. "Then will you keep your mouth shut?"

"Yes."

"For at least an hour?"

Half-George held up two fingers and solemnly swore. Tortot steered the donkey around a frozen pond. "I come from the valley of the Uncurious Folk."

"Yeah, yeah..."

"If you don't believe me..."

"No, no, I believe you," Half-George said quickly. "But why is it called that?"

"It's pretty obvious, isn't it?"

"So no one there is..."

"Exactly. Take the town crier. The man started when he was thirteen and now he's over seventy, but no one knows what he sounds like, not even now, because there's never any news. Or maybe there is news, but he doesn't want to tell anyone and the village doesn't want to hear it."

There was a quiet chuckle.

"Do you think I'm lying?" Tortot sniffed. "If you think I'm lying..."

"You're not lying, you're not lying," Half-George cried.

"In fact," Tortot continued after an offended silence, "everyone is so uncurious that when a villager goes to see the doctor with an ailment, the villager doesn't say anything and the doctor doesn't ask any questions. They just sit there, across the desk from each other, tapping their feet on the floor, humming a bit, and then they both go their own ways. And do you know what the funny thing is? The illness usually clears up after that, but the patient doesn't mention it and the doctor doesn't need to know."

"If you ask me," said Half-George, chuckling aloud now, "you're making it up as you go along."

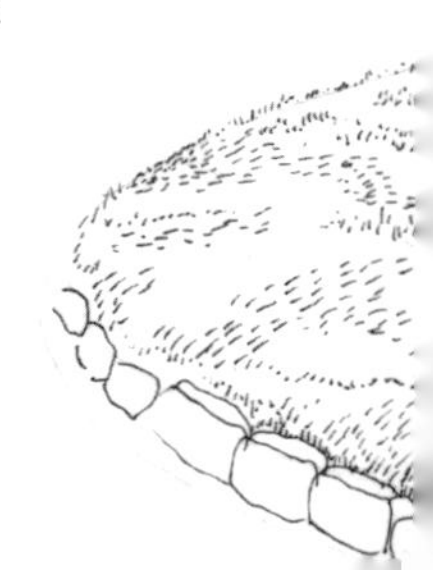

"Of course I am," said Tortot.

There was a contented yawn. Tortot did not need to glance around to see what the little half-soldier looked like. Like a caterpillar wrapped up in five blankets, with two damask tablecloths around his neck, and an old red tea cosy sliding down over his scrawny ears.

"So everything's crooked, eh?" said Half-George suddenly.

"Where?"

"In your village."

Tortot gazed at the waggling ears of his bespectacled donkey. Then he chased away a non-existent fly. "Where did you get that idea from?"

"You dream at night. Out loud."

"Dreams are lies," said Tortot, but somehow it did not sound entirely convincing.

"Don't you miss your village?"

"A few bricks, a hundred sheep, a broken village pump and a road that's so steep you tumble down it instead of walking? Nope."

There was a pause.

"If it were my village, I'd miss it," said Half-George.

"But it isn't your village."

For a while, Half-George didn't say anything else. There was enough to listen to. The musical creaking of the old cart, the crunch of the bespectacled donkey's hoofs in the snow, and the gentle breeze blowing through the treetops.

Twice they encountered a patrol. Both times, Tortot slammed the lid on the barrel, but no one stopped the field cook. The reputation of the Imperial Gherkin Barrel was sufficient. The weather was so cold that Tortot could no longer feel the reins in his hands, but that did not matter. His donkey seemed to sense exactly where he wanted to go.

At the end of the birch wood, the river began. It was so wide that the enemy tents on the opposite bank were no more than tiny pale-green triangles in the flat, white landscape. The river was still flowing. Pieces of ice the size of a meadow floated by in the wild grey-black water. A swan sat on one of them, hissing mournfully, one foot frozen to the ice.

"Tortot?"

"Mmm."

"Your herbs."

"What about my herbs?"

Half-George stared at him. The cook felt his face turning red. "Yes, halfwit, I'm well aware!" He turned the heel of his boot in the snow and swept away the top layer. Pale and puny blades of grass emerged.

"There are no fresh herbs in winter," said Half-George with a grin.

"Shut your mouth," said Tortot.

It was cold and icy and the war was in deep hibernation. The hussar on guard on the other side of the river, with his cap down low over his ears and his scarf pulled up high, could see hardly anything. The binoculars around his neck remained unused. He would not have been the first soldier whose eye sockets had frozen to the metal. If he had looked, though, he would have had a fine tale to get him through the dull winter days.

The story of the enemy cook who made a fire by the river, fried two eggs and fed one of them to a gherkin barrel.

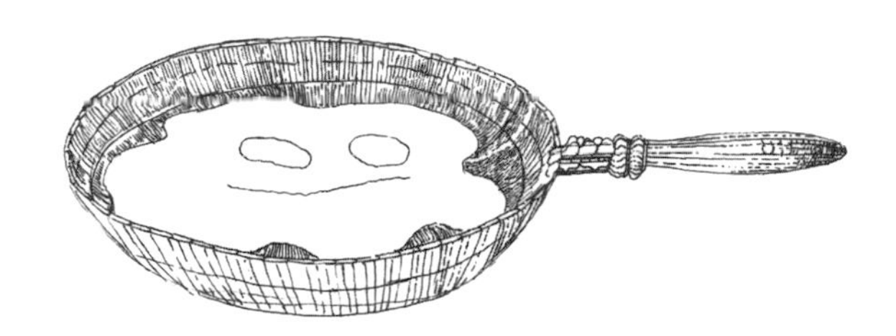

CHAPTER 15

The war is dead...

With the thaw and the beginning of spring, the war resumed. Soldiers broke loose like cows after a long winter. At exactly 9 a.m., they hurtled onto the agreed battlefield as if it were the juiciest pasture. Both sides came up with the most ingenious methods for doing each other in. The ingenuity of one camp or the other was often so impressive that the generals of the opposing side cheered and loudly clapped their gloved hands.

Credit where it is due, after all.

There were significant losses on both sides, but the armies of the Imperial Emperors had captured the river, which meant they had a ready supply of new soldiers, who were increasingly young boys of Half-George's age. What they were lacking in experience they more than made up for with their eagerness and enthusiasm. Every day the battle song descended over the fields like a choir of angels:

Hack, hack, hack,
chop the foe into the pot!
Whack, whack, whack,
let's cook him nice and hot!
Mash, mash, mash,
beat him up until he's dead!
Bash, bash, bash,
grind his bones to make my bread!
He is weak, we are strong,
and we sing a hero's song.
Hack, whack, bash, mash!
Hack, whack, bash, mash!
Wham! Bam! Dead!

A month and a half later, the very last army between the mountains and the sea was defeated. Seventy years had passed since the very first war of the Imperial Emperors; there had been so many losses that new mathematical models had to be devised in order to record the outcome of the battles, but the Imperial Emperors had succeeded in increasing their empire's territory threefold. All the land between the sea and the mountains now belonged to them.

Filled with melancholy, the generals cleared their maps. One by one, all the pins from all the manoeuvres were removed until the pin box was brimming over.

"Tortot! Tortot!" whispered Half-George.

"What?"

"The war is over. It's finally over! Do you know what that means?"

"That there's a new war brewing elsewhere?"

The Eternal Peace was signed. For a week, there were memorials and commemorations. There were memorials of commemorations and commemorations of memorials. Every ceremony was accompanied by endless speeches.

Then there was a lavish twenty-course banquet for the superior officers and spit-roasted chicken for the privates. Tortot worked himself into the ground, and Half-George had to pull out all the stops, too. But occasionally, between breakfast and lunch, between lunch and dinner, there was a little time.

"We'll be able to leave soon," Half-George said dreamily. "Just imagine..."

"Hmm."

"And you can go back to your village, can't you? Tortot?"

"What?"

"Would you mind if..."

"If what?"

"Oh, never mind."

"Okay, then," said Tortot. He gave Half-George up to the count of five. He got to three.

"Are there any barrels in your village, Tortot?"

Tortot pretended to ponder this question. "Not as far as I know."

Half-George winced in disappointment.

"But maybe?..." Tortot frowned. Half-George looked at him hopefully. Then the field cook shook his head. "No, that's not a barrel, it's a bucket. What do you want with a barrel anyway?"

Half-George chewed on the words, but they were as tough as an old piece of steak. "Well, um... I th... thought... th... that... I... um... maybe..."

"Oh, wait," said Tortot. He slapped his forehead. "How could I forget? There's a barrel at the bottom of my mother's garden. A bit smaller than the gherkin barrel. We used it to collect rainwater, but we haven't needed it since they dug the canal. I suppose you could have that."

Half-George beamed. "Have it? You mean that?... I-I-I could... A-And you?..."

"Of course," said Tortot generously. "Just give me your address and I'll make sure it's delivered."

No, it was not kind.

But Eternal Peace always made Tortot a little prickly.

CHAPTER 16

How Tortot's mother learned to postpone death

The war had made the crooked village sonless but for one son, and what a worthless son he was. If he made a table or a chair, you could bet that the legs would break within a couple of days, or that the son would accidentally nail himself to the piece of furniture. He was no good to anyone as a bricklayer either. The mortar he laid crumbled like dry oatmeal.

The only son wandered around the village, from one trade to the next.

The carpenter, the blacksmith, the mason, cobbler, gravedigger and baker—all of them put him to work and let him make a mess. Antoine the Butcher watched patiently as the boy boned meat as if he were blind. Tortot usually forgot to remove the membranes and left all the sinews in, so the whole village ended up chewing their jaws off on the tough bits of meat. Not to mention the dangerous splinters of bone that he overlooked.

But none of them sent him packing; they simply waited for him to resign, because the men did not want any trouble with their wives.

"Remember!" the women had said. "His mother's sadness is eightfold. Imagine if your heart were struck eight times. Imagine the devastation in her heart. So don't you dare fire that boy!"

"Tortot, put your coat on! You might think it's already spring, but it's not. Have you had your morning cup of tea? You don't want to get a bladder infection, not with your poor health. And don't forget you mustn't run, no matter how late you are. You don't want to go breaking a leg, not with your brittle bones. And watch out for that donkey in the blackberry patch. Don't walk behind it, you hear me? That animal is as sly as a viper."

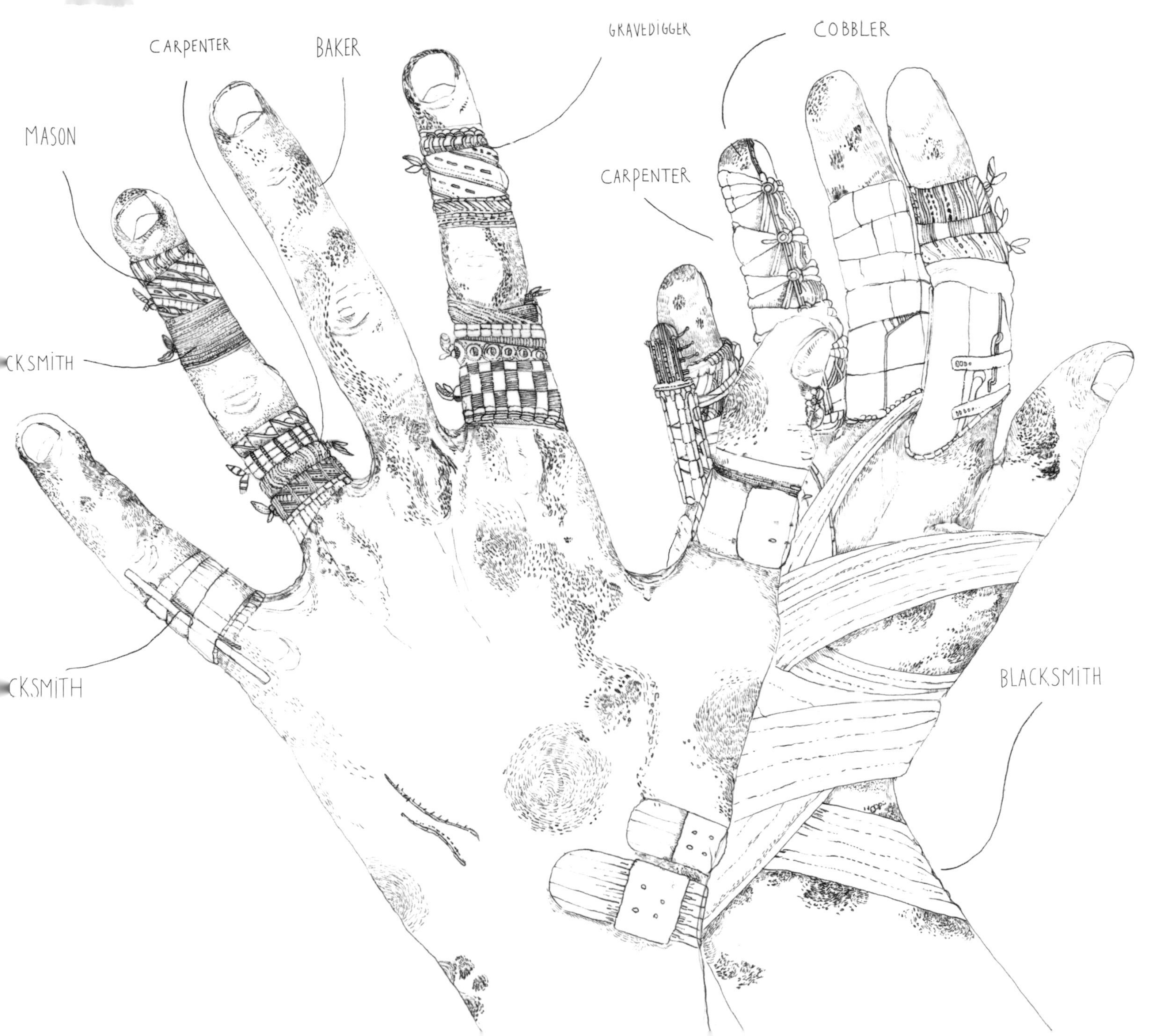
GRAVEDIGGER
COBBLER
CARPENTER
BAKER
MASON
CARPENTER
CKSMITH
CKSMITH
BLACKSMITH

She mothered him enough for nine.
Nine times the worry for just one son.

She had received official notification three times. The black-edged envelopes were still unopened on the mantelpiece.

One time, a trumpeter appeared at the door, a black plume on his hat.

"I have the unfortunate duty of informing you that during combat…"

She silenced him with a gesture. "I've heard enough."

"But don't you want to know which…"

"I know all I need to know, thank you."

"But, madam, it's my duty to…"

"Enough. Just play your trumpet."

Shaking his head, he reached into his case and pulled out a dented trumpet. He was an elderly trumpeter, with pince-nez spectacles and a grubby and crumpled uniform that hung loosely from his shoulders.

She never cried. Why should she? As long as she did not know which one had been killed, she could keep her sons alive. Not all of them at once, but in turns. One time the news would be about Bertrand or Jumeaux, another it would be Itrahim or Gerard. And when the grief came too close, she quickly let another one die instead.

And so she learned how to postpone death.

"Tortot? Tortot? I don't see what business you have going outside at this late hour. And why on earth are you walking around without a light? Next thing you know, you'll fall and it won't just be your brittle bones that'll finish you off. Just one little wound could give you blood poisoning. You'll swell up like a balloon, and don't go thinking I'll be able to put it right for you. Tortot? Tortot?"

One morning, so early that everyone was asleep, young Tortot turned his back on the village. He felt the windows of the houses like eyes on his back, but he saw no one. A dog was sleeping by the village pump. The creature was too old and decrepit to start barking.

Tortot fixed his eyes on the steep slope ahead and started walking. He did not look back, not at the beginning of the path and not as he passed the obelisk.

And that was how the last son left the village.

CHAPTER 17
... Long live the war!

The Imperial Emperors were still taking their gherkin baths. They had two large oak tubs filled with warm gherkin jelly and separated by a tall screen.

"If my poor face showed just a fraction of your radiant beauty, my dear Keflavik," one emperor called over the screen, "I would drown in bliss."

"But first I wish I could call a sliver of your youthful complexion my own, my dearest Husavik," the other emperor called back. "Then I should die of supreme happiness."

Opinions differ as to how the conflict began that went down in history as the War of the Gherkins and heralded the end of the Imperial Emperors' empire.

According to one version, one of the Imperial Emperors had not slept well because of an elusive flea and so he returned the other Imperial Emperor's compliment that morning in less glowing terms than usual.

Another story says that the footmen of either Husavik or Keflavik (the sources are contradictory) could not get the log fire under the tub to burn properly, whereupon Keflavik (or Husavik) had sniggered (according to the one emperor) or coughed (according to the other) and Husavik (or Keflavik) had accused Keflavik (or Husavik) of ordering his footmen to pee on the wood that morning, so the fire did not reach the right temperature and the healing properties of the gherkin jelly proved ineffective.

But the most likely explanation was, if possible, even more banal.

Who were the Imperial Emperors supposed to fight now that there was no enemy left?

The mascot of Tortot's army was the first victim of the War of the Gherkins—even though the poor old rooster was only doing what he had done for years. He was executed by firing squad early one morning for daring to crow beneath the flag of the Twin Emperors. By doing so (according to the army), the creature was expressing sympathy for the old regime, which was nothing less than high treason.

"Long live the emperor!" the men in the camp chanted in unison. And "Death to the emperor!"

Muskets fired away until they were empty. Beer was poured in huge amounts. Considering a new war had just broken out, with the old one only just over, everyone was in surprisingly high spirits.

Until confusion slowly crept into the camp.

Exactly which emperor were they talking about? Which one was supposed to live long? And which should drop dead on the spot?

Heated discussions broke out.

That same evening, the camp divided into two new camps which now felt as passionately about killing each other as they had once, before the War of Gherkins, felt about fighting side by side.

Gunfire and shouting, the clashing of swords. Half-George clung frantically to his barrel.

"What *is* that?" he asked. "What *is* that?"

"The end of the Eternal Peace," was all Tortot replied. He poured the Eternal Soup back into the flask. Then he drove his bespectacled donkey and the cart into the tent and calmly began to sort out and load up his belongings.

Yet he was not as calm as he appeared. Just as some people have a faithful weather-predicting toe, Tortot had always had a perfect nose for war—but this war had taken him by surprise.

"Oh no! What are we going to do? What are we going to do?" cried Half-George.

"A good start would be to stop saying things twice," Tortot snapped back at him.

His thoughts were moving quickly. This chaos could work in his favour. It would soon be dark and that would be his best chance.

In all his years of war, the field cook had learned to keep his eyes open. So he knew that the guard post on the northern side of the camp was its weakest point. Beyond there, the river's marshy floodplain began, which had been swarming with night mosquitoes since spring. The itching from their bites could last for weeks and many a soldier had collapsed in a frenzy of scratching.

So most of the guards at that post did not spend all night there, but patrolled up and down.

As the first bullet whistled past, narrowly missing the tent, Tortot's donkey just twitched its ears and stared mournfully at the field cook through its spectacles.

Tortot took his herbs and wrapped them in a cloth. Much to his regret, he had to leave the herb cabinet behind, along with a stack of pots and pans. And he could not take his beloved camp bed either.

Half-George studied his movements as if trying to memorize them.

"What are you doing?"

"Leaving."

Half-George's eyes widened in fear. "You're n... You won't... You can't... l-leave me..."

"Of course not," said Tortot, "you just hide away in your barrel and don't move a muscle, not even if all hell breaks loose."

Before the half-soldier had a chance to stutter his thanks or, worse, to start snivelling, Tortot closed the lid and rolled the barrel onto the cart. Finally, he took down his tent.

Tortot was unlucky. The guards were at their post. The two were brothers, and Tortot knew them vaguely. Not exactly bright, each with half a brain, but clever enough together. He would have to be careful.

"What's that?" one of them asked.

"You can see for yourself, can't you?" said the other.

"I can see that I can see it, but can you see it too?"

"Long live the one emperor! Death to the other!" cried Tortot.

They looked at him suspiciously.

"Who says you want the same emperor dead as us?" one of them asked, irritably slapping his neck.

"And who says you wish the same emperor good health?" said the other, frantically scratching the back of his head.

The brothers aimed their muskets at Tortot.

"Ah, yes," said Tortot, putting his hands in the air and trying not to feel them falling prey to all those angry insects. "I understand. These are strange times. Who can you still trust? The general has deserted. Your best friend promises you eternal loyalty but then, as soon as your back's turned, he stabs you with a rapier. Why would you trust a simple cook? Someone who has provided you with food and drink every day? I completely understand. Times are so strange that you could believe anything of anyone. Take the two of you, for instance."

The guards looked at each other vacantly.

"Brothers, actual blood brothers!" Tortot cried passionately. "If you can't even trust your own brother, who can you trust? But if I wanted to speak ill of anyone in these strange times, it wouldn't be too difficult."

The guards blinked, as if they were excavating Tortot's words one by one, uncovering them and examining them, but no, they had already lost the thread.

"Well," continued Tortot. "You can, of course, decide that I am the enemy."

He paused for a few seconds to let his words sink in. "But I'm not the one who's standing here beside my own brother with a loaded gun."

Even after seven ordinary wars, two civil wars, three revolutions and two counter-revolutions, Tortot was still impressed by how subtly suspicion did its work. He saw both brothers stiffen.

It probably helped that, at that moment, a musket went off nearby. Even before the gunsmoke had cleared, Tortot had already led the donkey cart past the post.

"Tortot!"

Tortot turned around.

A fire had broken out near the gunpowder magazine. The camp was bathed in an eerie glow. There was not a breath of wind. The trees in the forest had transformed into enormous black claws, helplessly reaching up to the sky. He heard cries, the clashing of swords, shots.

"Tortot!"

The trees spewed forth a figure. This inky-black silhouette came limping towards the field cook, with rapier raised.

"Tortot!"

Tortot stood perfectly still, in the moon shadow of a huge oak. As long as he did not move, Crookleg would not see him, he was sure of that.

Did hate give off a smell? Or if you hated someone, did that allow you to sniff them out? Tortot had no idea, but Crookleg was making straight for him, like a hunting dog. The field cook searched in his apron for his knife, but did not find it. Quietly cursing, he braced himself. He was reluctant to get into a fight, as his skills clearly lay elsewhere, but if he had to, then he would.

But just as Crookleg came within a stone's throw of Tortot, there was a huge explosion. Tortot was thrown back against his cart and when he stood up again he saw devastation all around: fallen trees and ripped-off branches. There was no sign of the sergeant.

Tortot did not stop to think for a moment, but jumped onto his cart and headed into the marsh.

Although the field cook had known the journey would be difficult, he had underestimated the peril of the undertaking. The bespectacled donkey ploughed onwards across the increasingly swampy ground, panting like a pair of bellows. The moon had come up by then, but Tortot could barely make out his hand in front of his face. The mosquitoes swarmed around him like a stinging fog.

As the crow flies, the distance to the river was no more than two miles, but it took him more than three hours to reach it. And that was more by luck than judgement. By sunrise, the little donkey was trudging out of the marsh and up the steep embankment. The poor animal was covered in mud all the way up to its spectacles and Tortot's eyes were so swollen that he could hardly see anything, let alone steer the donkey.

"Shall I?..." asked Half-George.

If there had been any peasants working on the land, they would have had a good story to tell. The tale of a blind cook and of a barrel steering a bespectacled donkey.

But most of the villages had been burnt to the ground or shot to pieces, and the peasants had left. The fields were no good to anyone, having been poisoned by years of saltpetre and sulphur raining down on them and by the lead in the bullets. All around lay bloated corpses of rabbits, sparrows, crows and blackbirds, their stiff legs straight up in the air.

Although the land was devastated, the roads were well maintained. The army had regularly covered the muddy tracks with brushwood, sand and coal ash to assist the transportation of military equipment to the area. Tortot dozed off while Half-George got the bespectacled donkey to press on along the winding path.

"Look!" Half-George cried in delight. "Look, Tortot!"

The first thing the field cook noticed was that the musical creaking and squeaking of the cart had stopped. He struggled to open his eyes. He did not know exactly how long he had slept, but it must be late afternoon. The sun was more than halfway across the sky.

The cart stopped. Half-George shook his arm. "Just look at that!" he said, pointing.

A small field, half hidden in a dip. Swallows swooped and swirled, weaving in strings across the sky. Here was a place where the war had never been, where there had never been any shooting or fighting. Tortot was certain of that. This was a field that, in its sheltered position, had simply been overlooked.

But that was not why he suddenly felt something unfamiliar welling up in the corner of his eye, although it could have been the wind, or an allergic reaction to the mosquito bites.

Flowers waved among the corn. And not just any old flowers.

"Are those?..." asked Half-George breathlessly. "Is that?..."

Tortot was too stunned to reply.

The golden-purple king poppy made the field light and dark at the same time. As the wind blew through the corn, the delicate flowers bent deeply, disappeared for a moment, but then stood proudly upright once again, petals fluttering open and closed like butterfly wings.

That evening, they set up camp in the reed beds. They ate a hunk of bread with a scrap of cheese. Tortot did not want to make a fire. The area seemed deserted, but it was better to be safe than sorry. Besides, the ground was wet, so close to the river, and it was unlikely he would even manage to light a fire.

Tortot put up his tent. He picked armfuls of reeds and laid them on the boggy ground. Sadly, he thought back to his camp bed.

The tent flap was open. They looked out and watched the bespectacled donkey for a while as it plucked blades of grass from among the reeds with its precise lips.

"We should have stayed on the Lounging Lawn," said Half-George.

Even before dusk, the river mist was already spreading out across the land. Poplars were cut off from their roots, and the bespectacled donkey floated legless above the ground. Tortot closed the tent flap and wrapped himself in his blanket.

"Tortot..."

"Mmm."

"What if we come back here one day and what if there's peace and..."

"'What if' is in the graveyard. Next to 'Maybe' and..."

"'Eternal Peace'," Half-George continued, as if Tortot had said nothing. "You know, not just any old Eternal Peace, but, um... *Eternal* Eternal Peace. Then do you promise we can go back to the Lounging Lawn one day?"

"You know my promises are no good to you, don't you?"

"Of course," said Half-George, giving him a cautious grin. For the first time, Tortot noticed that he had a crooked tooth with a brown speckle on it. Why had he never noticed it before?

"But will you promise anyway?"

"Hmm..."

"Well?"

Tortot raised his hands in the air. Half-George's smile grew so wide that it almost went skittering off his face. Then, his expression suddenly deadly serious, he reached out, and what else could Tortot do but shake the little half-soldier's hand?

"Tortot?"

"What is it this time?!"

"Is everything in your village really that crooked?"

"Were your brothers deaf?"

"What do you mean?"

"All these questions of yours! These never-ending questions!"

But it was already late. And no matter how exhausted Tortot was, sleep would not come. Besides, what was the night for if not for stories?

"Crooked?" he said. "That's putting it mildly! We have shoes with special heels. They're so high at the back that when you're walking uphill, it seems as if you're still on level ground."

"What about if you're going downhill?"

"That's the really clever thing about them. There's a screw in the middle. It lets you swivel the heel so that the high part is at the front."

"It's a pity I don't have any legs now," said Half-George.

Tortot was silent.

"Will you tell me another recipe?" asked the half-soldier, fighting his exhaustion.

"Go to sleep," said Tortot.

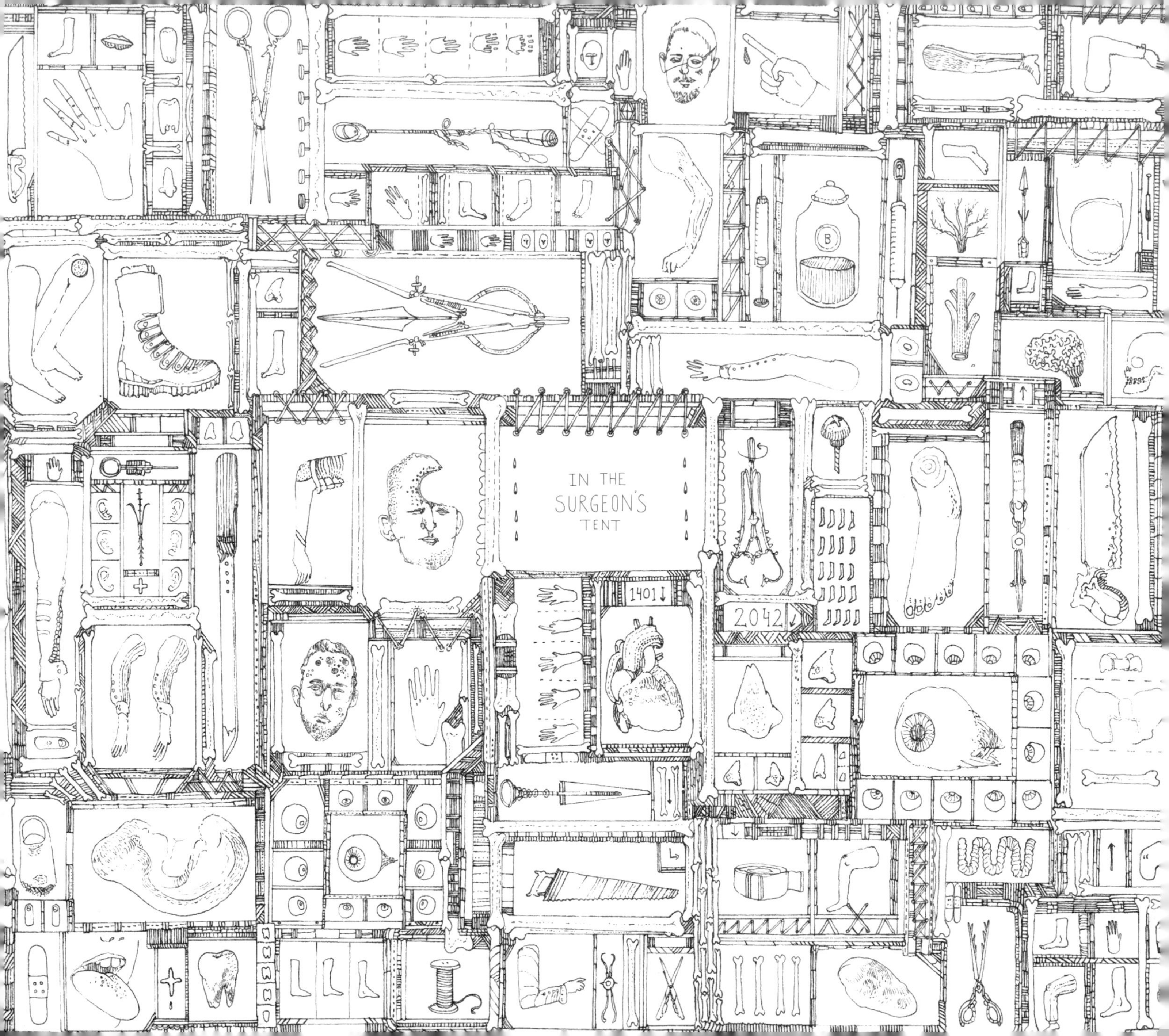

IN THE
SURGEON'S
TENT
1401
2042
B

CHAPTER 18

In which the army goes in search of itself

There is no protocol for an army that is fighting itself. Or perhaps there is, but during the War of the Gherkins no one had time to look it up, let alone follow it. There were no starting times anymore, or designated battlefields. All the rules about strategy and the use of weapons had been thrown overboard too.

At the strangest times, in the oddest places and without any guidelines at all, the two half-armies eagerly started hacking away at each other, slicing, stabbing and shooting.

Within just three hours, the surgeon had so many body parts in his tent that he could easily have assembled a new army.

If one of the two camps had not captured the armoury, where the weapons and cannons were stored, they probably would have gone on until no man was left standing.

The losing half-army decided to retreat. Hmm, retreat... It was more like running away as fast as they could... Part of the half-army ended up in the marsh during their escape. This turned out badly for the cavalry in particular. With their weapons and armour, half of them drowned, horses and all.

As if that were not bad enough, the halved army then divided into two quarters. This happened in the Unholy Woods, a place to the west of the camp, famous for its will-o'-the-wisps, tangled paths, tracks that forked and forks that split.

Before they knew what was happening, one quarter had lost the other quarter.

The first quarter-army wandered aimlessly through the woods for hours. The second chanced upon a way out, and marched onwards across the poisoned fields beside the river.

The distance between the separated quarter-armies could easily have grown so large that they never found each other again, but then the Poker Player, in the second quarter-army, got a nasty stone in his boot. It would normally have been removed in an instant, were it not for the fact that the colonel was wearing extremely complicated armour.

Relieving him of his armour was a time-consuming activity at the best of times, but the quarter-army suffered further delays when the colonel ordered all the soldiers to plant their lances and spears in the soil to make a circle around him and then to lie on the ground with their faces down.

This was not just for the sake of modesty.

What no one knew (or so he thought) was that he was incontinent—the result of an unfortunate sword fight in the battle against the Breidelian army. He always wore a nappy sprinkled with a scent made from magnolia flowers.

The colonel had no idea that everyone in the army knew about his incontinence (in fact, they secretly called him Colonel Williewasher instead of Colonel Nilliewasser).

Over an hour had passed by the time the Poker Player had got undressed and dressed again, and the stone had been removed.

During that hour, the other quarter-army had taken a tangled and twisted route through the Unholy Woods and had become more lost than ever.

Or at least that was what they thought.

What they did not realize was that several times they had been less than ten yards from the edge of the forest. If Fairface had not happened to knock his brother Crookleg down a woody hillock—just as their father finished getting dressed in his changing room of spears and lances—they could probably have gone on wandering for days.

Fairface had walked up the slope. Not because he imagined that he would find a way out (the place was teeming with woody hillocks and they all looked infuriatingly alike), but to prove that he was still in charge. Mutiny could easily break out in such circumstances.

Crookleg had followed his brother. When he had reached the top of the slope, he asked if the army should also follow them.

Startled, Fairface, who had been deep in thought, swiftly turned around and knocked his brother down the hill with his swagger stick.

Crookleg went rolling down the slope like a snowball, bumping into beeches, birches, oaks, and tumbling through blackberry bushes, stinging nettles and other hostile undergrowth before disappearing from sight with a shrill cry. He left a tunnel of green behind him, and when the major followed his brother's trail, he suddenly, as if it were some kind of trick, found himself walking out of the woods and into a large open field.

At that point, the separated quarter-armies were less than two miles apart. The river landscape was flat, and there were no trees or buildings nearby, so sound would normally carry a long way. Under ordinary circumstances, missing each other here would have been quite some feat.

If only the fog had not been so thick.

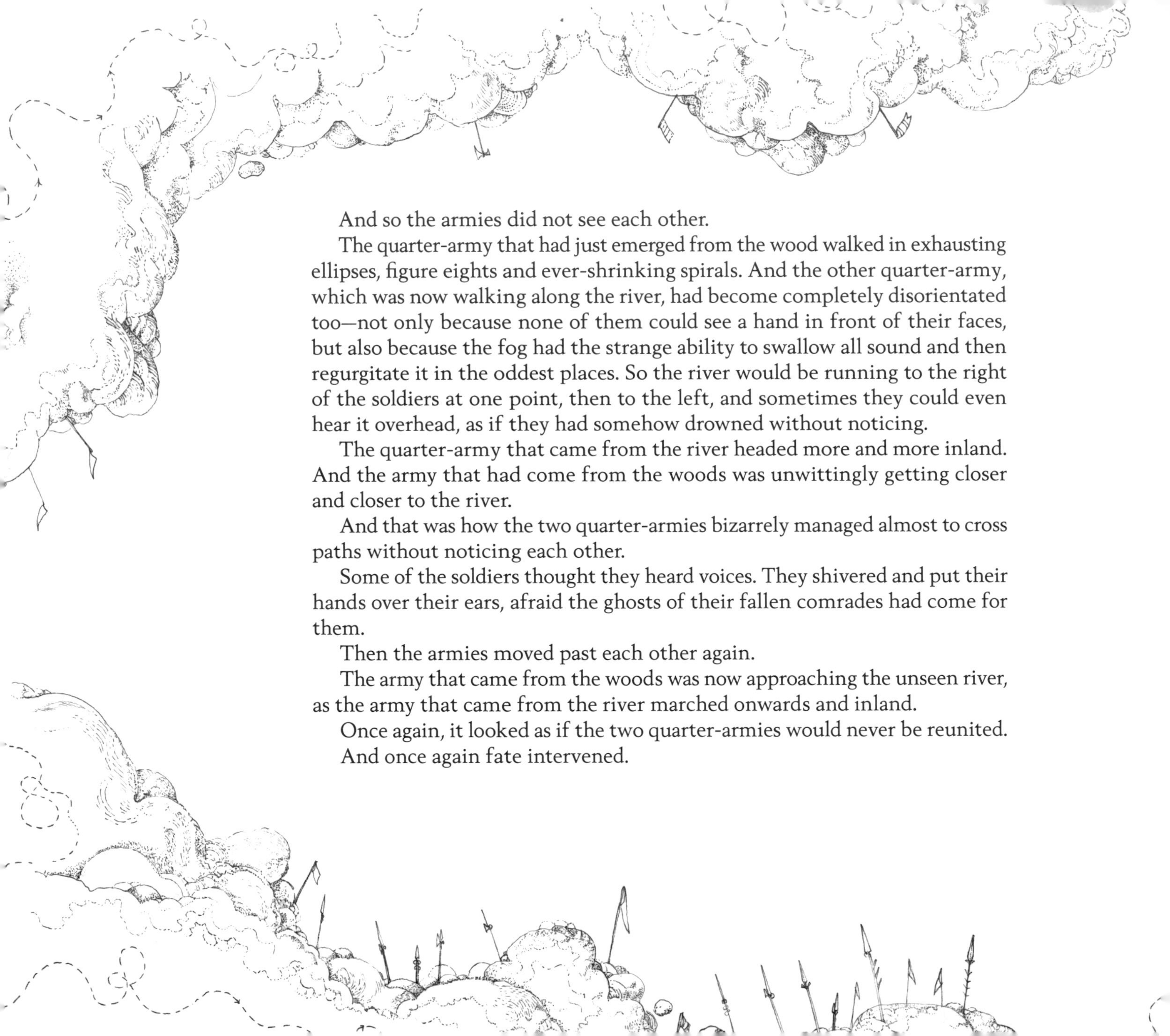

And so the armies did not see each other.

The quarter-army that had just emerged from the wood walked in exhausting ellipses, figure eights and ever-shrinking spirals. And the other quarter-army, which was now walking along the river, had become completely disorientated too—not only because none of them could see a hand in front of their faces, but also because the fog had the strange ability to swallow all sound and then regurgitate it in the oddest places. So the river would be running to the right of the soldiers at one point, then to the left, and sometimes they could even hear it overhead, as if they had somehow drowned without noticing.

The quarter-army that came from the river headed more and more inland. And the army that had come from the woods was unwittingly getting closer and closer to the river.

And that was how the two quarter-armies bizarrely managed almost to cross paths without noticing each other.

Some of the soldiers thought they heard voices. They shivered and put their hands over their ears, afraid the ghosts of their fallen comrades had come for them.

Then the armies moved past each other again.

The army that came from the woods was now approaching the unseen river, as the army that came from the river marched onwards and inland.

Once again, it looked as if the two quarter-armies would never be reunited.

And once again fate intervened.

With the first army, it was a herd of young wild bulls that forced a change of direction. And in the second army, a hussar accidentally poked his lance into a wasps' nest that was hanging in a tree.

And so it happened that the quarter-armies veered closer again and, at the crack of dawn, finally happened upon each other, in spite of the dense fog, in a spot not far from the river.

Right in the reed beds where Tortot had pitched his tent.

CHAPTER 19

In which the formidable Tortot undoes his desertion

The field cook, who even in his deepest sleep had always had an exceptional ear for impending doom, did not notice until it was too late. The quarter-army led by Nilliewasser the Poker Player loomed up out of the fog, to the left of the tent. Less than a minute later, the other quarter-army emerged on the other side, following Nilliewasser the Fair.

The field cook had just enough time to slam the lid firmly on the gherkin barrel. He knew the game was up.

In those days, any ignoramus could have told you the punishment for desertion.

If you were lucky, you would be hanged, drawn and quartered or tied to the barrel of a cannon and a hole would be shot through your torso. If you were unlucky, you were boiled alive.

Was it because Tortot had slept so badly? Because he realized that his arts of culinary seduction were useless without ingredients to make a meal? Or because the poison under his chef's hat would never be enough to do away with half an army?

Whatever it was, for the first time in his entire life, Tortot had nothing prepared.

No words, no meals, no poison, nothing.

And for the first time he noticed his knees almost knocking with fear.

So he was astonished when the soldiers of the two quarter-armies greeted one another enthusiastically without showing any particular interest in him. They simply put up their tents. The colonel walked past Tortot, patted him absent-mindedly on the shoulder and began swapping stories with the major about all that had happened since they had been parted.

The confusion in Tortot's head clumped together like badly stirred Béchamel sauce. Why did they not arrest him for desertion? Had he turned into a ghost? Was this a dream? Some strange trick?

It was only when he overheard the conversations of the soldiers that he began to piece things together. And, even with his vivid imagination, Half-George had trouble believing what had happened when he heard the story later.

"So when the half-army ran away... There was so much panic and chaos that no one had time to inspect the troops?"

"Exactly."

"But what about later? When the one quarter lost the other quarter? Shouldn't they have noticed you weren't with them?"

"Yes, but the one quarter thought I was with the other. And vice versa. Or rather, they didn't think anything at first. But when they found each other at the spot where my tent was standing, they naturally assumed I'd been with the other quarter all that time."

"But no one would believe that," said Half-George.

And yet that was what happened.

Tortot had a brief moment of worry when he suddenly felt a finger jabbing into his back. He turned and found himself staring into Crookleg's furious face.

Crookleg looked as if he'd been fighting for a year in the very thick of the battle.

His uniform was scorched, his eyebrows were singed from the explosion in the gunpowder magazine, his mouth and left eye were swollen by a dozen wasp stings, and the right-hand side of his face was black and blue after his involuntary collision with an oak tree.

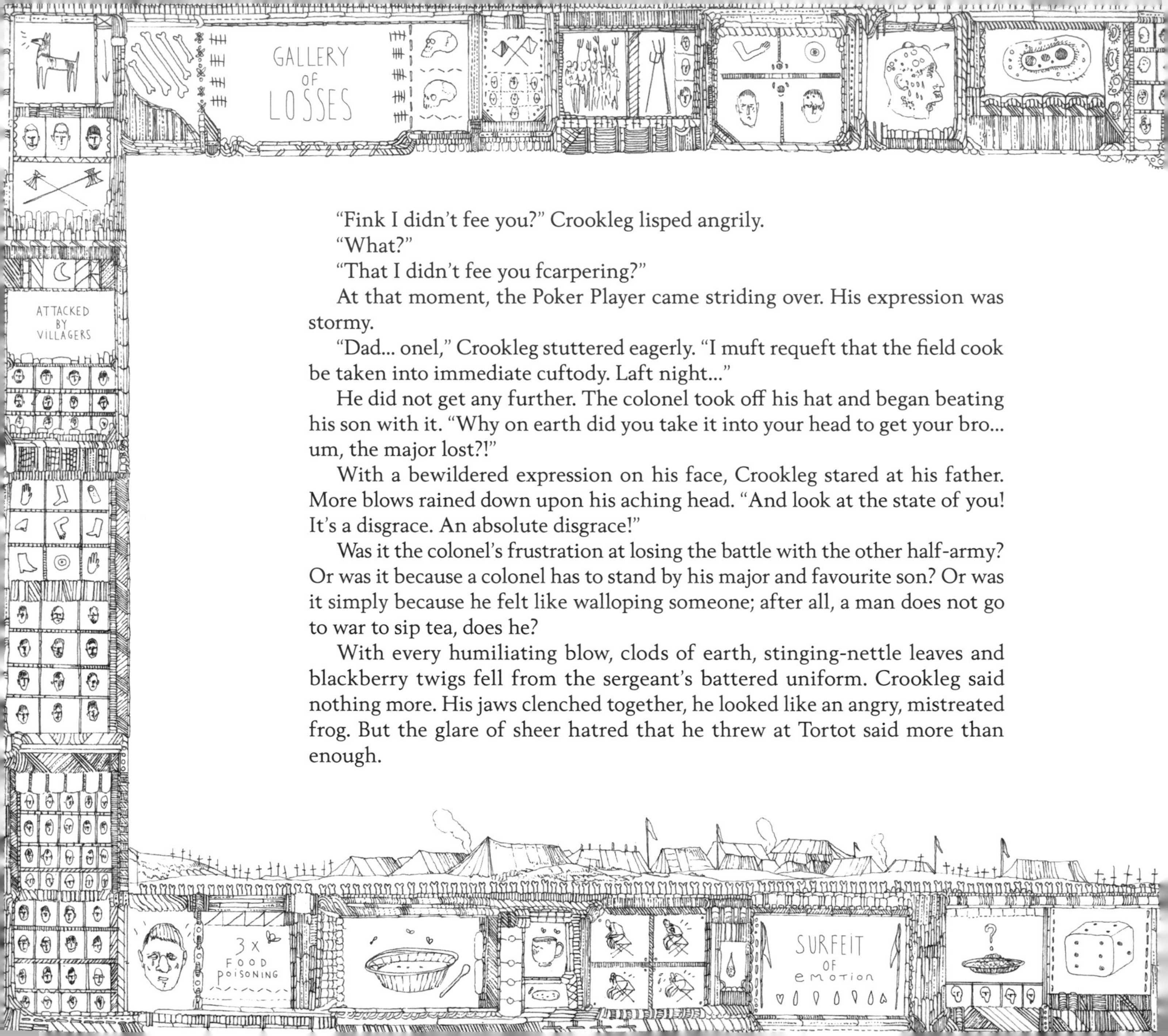

"Fink I didn't fee you?" Crookleg lisped angrily.

"What?"

"That I didn't fee you fcarpering?"

At that moment, the Poker Player came striding over. His expression was stormy.

"Dad... onel," Crookleg stuttered eagerly. "I muft requeft that the field cook be taken into immediate cuftody. Laft night..."

He did not get any further. The colonel took off his hat and began beating his son with it. "Why on earth did you take it into your head to get your bro... um, the major lost?!"

With a bewildered expression on his face, Crookleg stared at his father. More blows rained down upon his aching head. "And look at the state of you! It's a disgrace. An absolute disgrace!"

Was it the colonel's frustration at losing the battle with the other half-army? Or was it because a colonel has to stand by his major and favourite son? Or was it simply because he felt like walloping someone; after all, a man does not go to war to sip tea, does he?

With every humiliating blow, clods of earth, stinging-nettle leaves and blackberry twigs fell from the sergeant's battered uniform. Crookleg said nothing more. His jaws clenched together, he looked like an angry, mistreated frog. But the glare of sheer hatred that he threw at Tortot said more than enough.

For half a year, the half-army wandered around. Other than the few weapons they had taken, they had little to defend themselves with. And an army without any weapons worth mentioning is no more than a horde of vagabonds. At best, the locals merely tolerated the ragged, wandering army.

But sometimes they chased them away with clubs, pitchforks or dogs.

Summer came and went.

Strangely, there was no trace of the other half-army. They seemed to have vanished into thin air. There were no more clashes and skirmishes.

Not that the danger was any less, though.

In the autumn, a virus spread through the half-army, wiping out a fifth of the men. One night in December, the Poker Player's army was attacked by a large band of robbers, who were after the few weapons that the army still had. And just before spring began, a rickety suspension bridge collapsed and five men went tumbling into the ravine below.

"A man does not need a war," said the Poker Player grimly, shuffling his well-thumbed poker cards. "Give him a chasm and a virus and that is soon the end of that."

Whether a man needed a war or not, after that period of six months the rusty war machine began to move again. And with more energy than ever before. This was partly because of the Imperial Emperors' unquenched thirst for power, and partly because of the occupied counties, duchies and city-states themselves.

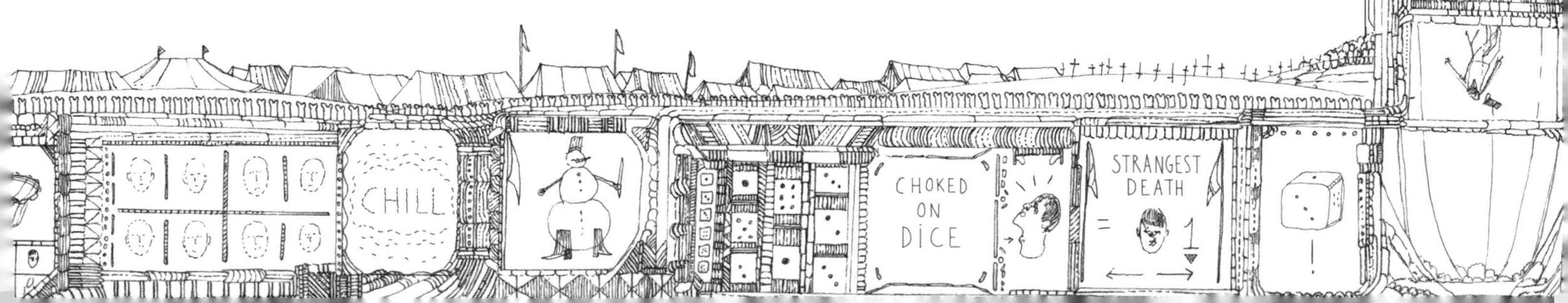

Now that the power of the Twin Emperors had been broken, they smelled a chance to win back their captured territories.

All they had to do was choose the side of the emperor who had the greatest chance of victory. An extremely delicate game began.

Meetings were convened, vetoes issued, spies sent out, counter-spies unmasked, pacts forged and then broken.

Ultimately—how predictable!—about half of the parties chose one emperor and the other half chose the other.

A new war began to grow.

A war that would develop into a conflict that, in its violence and horror, would far surpass Half-George's nightmares.

"We're never going to get out of the war," said Half-George miserably.

"That's right. You go on thinking that way."

"Eternal Peace doesn't exist."

"No, of course it doesn't!" was what Tortot wanted to shout, but instead he heard himself saying that just because the Eternal Peace had happened to fail on this occasion, it was no reason to start wailing. "If everyone sat around moping at the slightest bit of difficulty, well..."

But Half-George was right. The number of guards had tripled since the beginning of this latest war. Not a flea could get in or out of the camp unnoticed now, let alone a cook and a child soldier.

There were no chances for escape during the daily marches either. Crookleg made sure of that. He always rode directly behind Tortot and did not allow him out of his sight for a moment.

The war would not let them go and Tortot knew it. But sometimes knowing something did you no good—and someone else constantly reminding you about it did you even less good.

Thank goodness his work had become a lot more challenging. Now that the sutlers had run off (you can't pluck a bald chicken), scraping meals together was a full day's work for Tortot. He had to bargain with grumpy, greedy farmers and it took all his creativity to turn his slim pickings into something resembling an acceptable meal. But that was a welcome change from Half-George's misery.

"What if there's war everywhere soon, Tortot?" said the young soldier. "What if there's nowhere peaceful left in the entire world, like in my dream? What if..."

"How many times do I have to tell you," Tortot answered sharply. "'What if' is in the graveyard, next to 'Maybe' and 'Imagine'."

At night the field cook dreamed. Not about his mother or the little crooked house and the lizards falling from the wall with a soft thud, but about a swan floating along an icy river, its black foot firmly frozen to a block of ice.

CHAPTER 20

About creative warfare

In the first few months, the fighting spread like wildfire across the land between the mountains and the sea. The armies marched from east to west, from north to south. They often covered tens of miles a day, with hardly any time to sleep or even to put up their tents. The supplies sometimes did not arrive for days and in the chaos of who was on which side, exhausted units came to blows, losing hundreds of men, only to discover at the end of the battle that they were from allied lands.

It was not the Imperial Emperors who put an end to this disgrace, but the supreme generals of both sides. They were scared to death that they would have no men left if this "War of the Headless Chickens", as the disgruntled soldiers had dubbed it, did not come to a stop soon. At an ultra-secret summit meeting, they decided on a clearly defined war zone.

The victims of this summit were the cities of Blät and Vladzimka, one the capital of the free state of Horden, the other of its neighbour, Old Arcadia.

Both were border cities and, as the crow flies, no more than ten miles apart.

For centuries, Blät and Vladzimka had been prosperous cities with lively trading activity, a joint army and family ties so tightly entangled that whenever two sweethearts wanted to marry, it took the archivist a month to comb through yards of historical records and ensure there was no unauthorized entwining of bloodlines.

But that time was over.

The armies were redeployed and positioned around both cities. The army that Tortot served ended up in Blät, while the other army descended upon

Vladzimka. The two emperors, who, as a result of the generals' careful manoeuvring, had decided that this city war was their own idea, were both hoping for a swift victory.

Fierce attacks followed. The Poker Player would attack Vladzimka, almost bringing the city to its knees, and then the enemy army would carry out such aggressive charges that Blät could be saved only by the skin of its teeth. It was an agonizingly tough tug-of-war, the likes of which had never been seen before.

Tortot was placed in charge of the kitchen at the convent in Blät, which was not far from the officers' quarters. The kitchen was in the basement and it was equipped with a large wood-fired oven and plenty of pots and pans.

"But that's not all," Tortot told Half-George. "We also have thick walls, bars on the windows and..."

He presented the big rusty key to the boy. "Now we don't need to worry about some Nilliewasser or other bursting in."

Half-George smiled, but there was too much sadness in his eyes to believe that smile. "I don't think Nilliewasser is our biggest problem," he said.

There was the dull thud of a cannonball impact, far off, but close enough to lend force to Half-George's words.

This latest war was the work of strategists who had graduated from the most modern, recently established military academy and who worked for both camps. They were as wily as weasels and as precise as Swiss clockwork. Their atrocities were scrutinized to the tiniest detail, mathematically complex, supremely well organized and twice as effective as the atrocities of wars gone by.

Meanwhile, the arms industry had also been busy. The old-fashioned siege guns with their twenty-four-pound balls had been exchanged for cannons that could fire two balls linked by a chain, which very effectively cut down pikemen who were marching in a square formation.

Then there were the hail bombs: wooden shells filled with lead bullets, which scattered like hail when they were fired and could mow down half a company at once.

One particularly notorious projectile was the steam-ball, a bomb that spewed great clouds of poisonous smoke on impact, which made the enemy so sick that they fell to the ground gagging and offered no further resistance.

But there were other, even more creative ways to get the better of the enemy...

A heavily guarded convent near Vladzimka, which was known to have underground stores of saltpetre and sulphur, the soul and the spirit of gunpowder, was captured without a struggle. The nuns who lived there were said to have given the enemy a particularly warm welcome.

The next morning, one of the conquerors saw a nun wriggling out through a refectory window in her birthday suit, cursing like a sailor. She had a rose tattooed on her thigh.

The refectory was full of nuns' habits.

The real nuns were found in the cellar, all tied together and as naked as the day they were born.

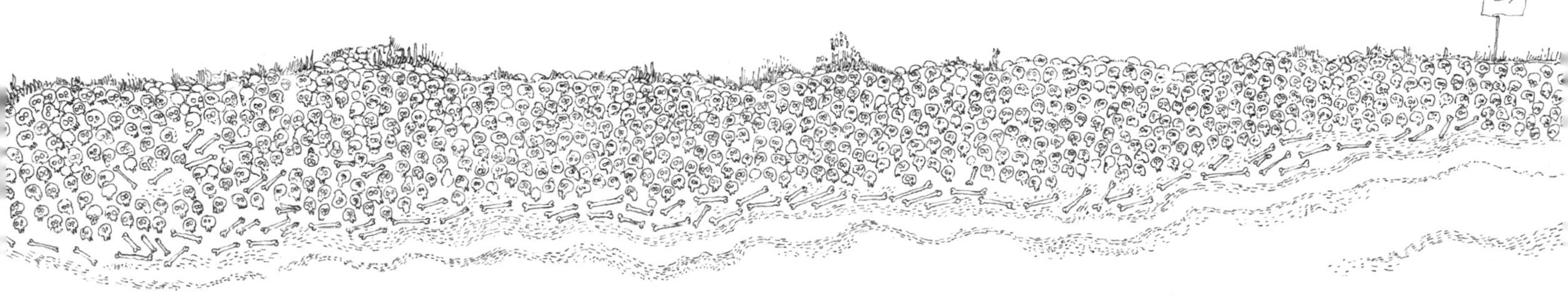

A few weeks later, the soldiers' hair began to fall out and then they developed high fevers.

Half of them went blind.

Syphilis as a weapon—it was certainly inventive.

But no matter how cunning and modern the warfare, two years later they reached a deadlock. So many men had died on both sides that you could walk across the fields from Blät to Vladzimka without touching the ground. All you had to do was step from one skull to the next, like stepping stones in a river.

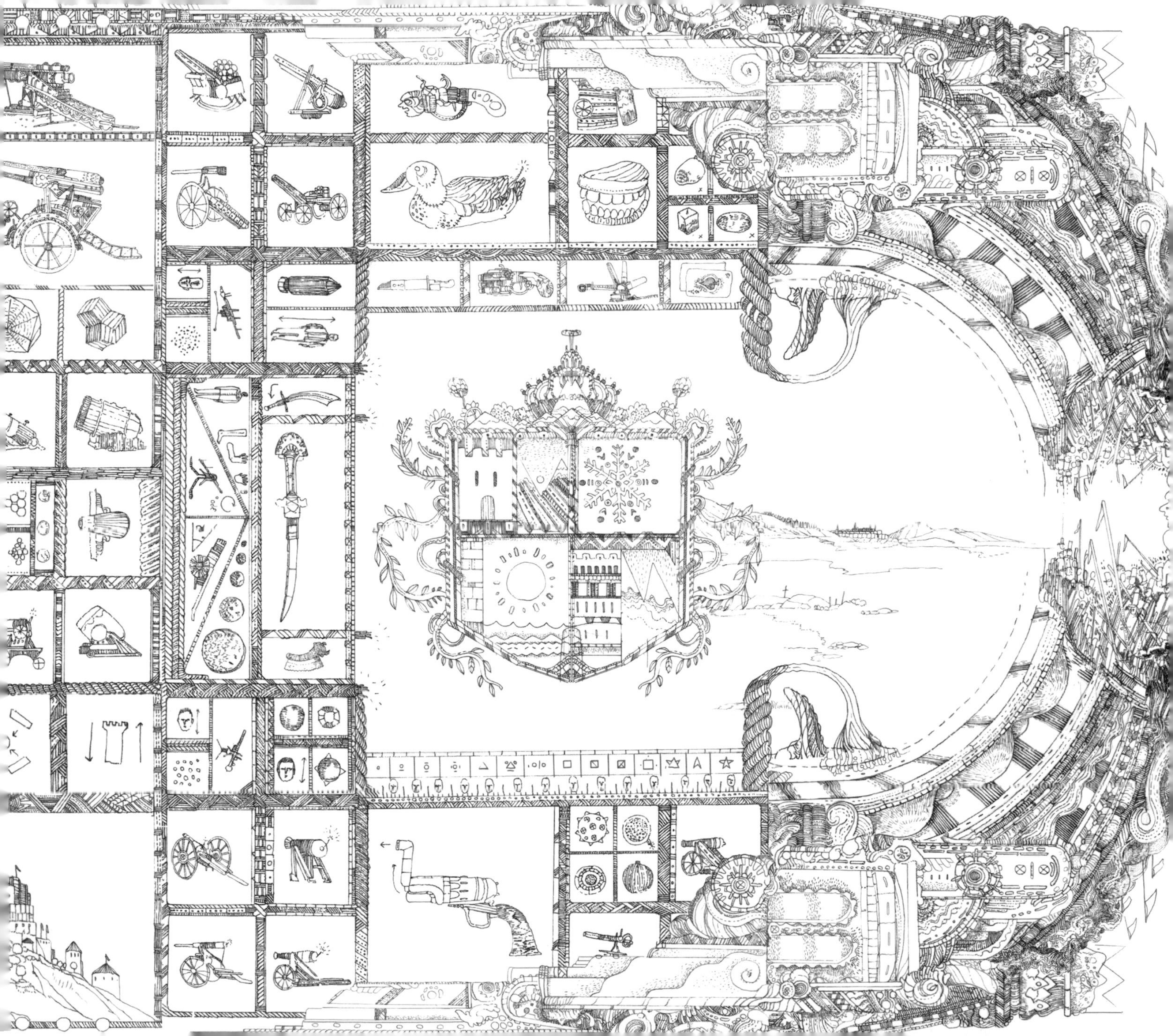

CHAPTER 21

In which Tortot makes a disturbing discovery

"Half-George?"

A quiet groan came from the barrel.

"Wake up."

Silence.

"Hey, sleepyhead!"

More silence from the barrel. Then Tortot thought he heard gentle snoring. Heavens above, how much sleep could a person take? Tortot whacked the barrel with his ladle and the half-soldier's startled head popped up.

"If you keep your eyes closed for too long, they'll stay that way. Did your mother never tell you that?"

Half-George looked at him dozily.

"Not to mention what too much dreaming does to your head! Too many dreams and it'll explode. A bomb's got nothing on it. Everyone knows that. I assume your brothers gave you practical advice as well as stories, didn't they? Well?"

In the past, Half-George had needed little encouragement to become an unstoppable chatterbox. Tortot could not remember how many times he had prayed—silently or at the top of his voice—for the boy to keep his mouth shut just for a moment, but now his silence was really getting to Tortot. And he reacted by talking for two.

"Let's see. Where did I leave my cleaver? I had it here just now. Isn't that just typical! *Saint Anthony, Saint Anthony, please take a look around. My knife is*

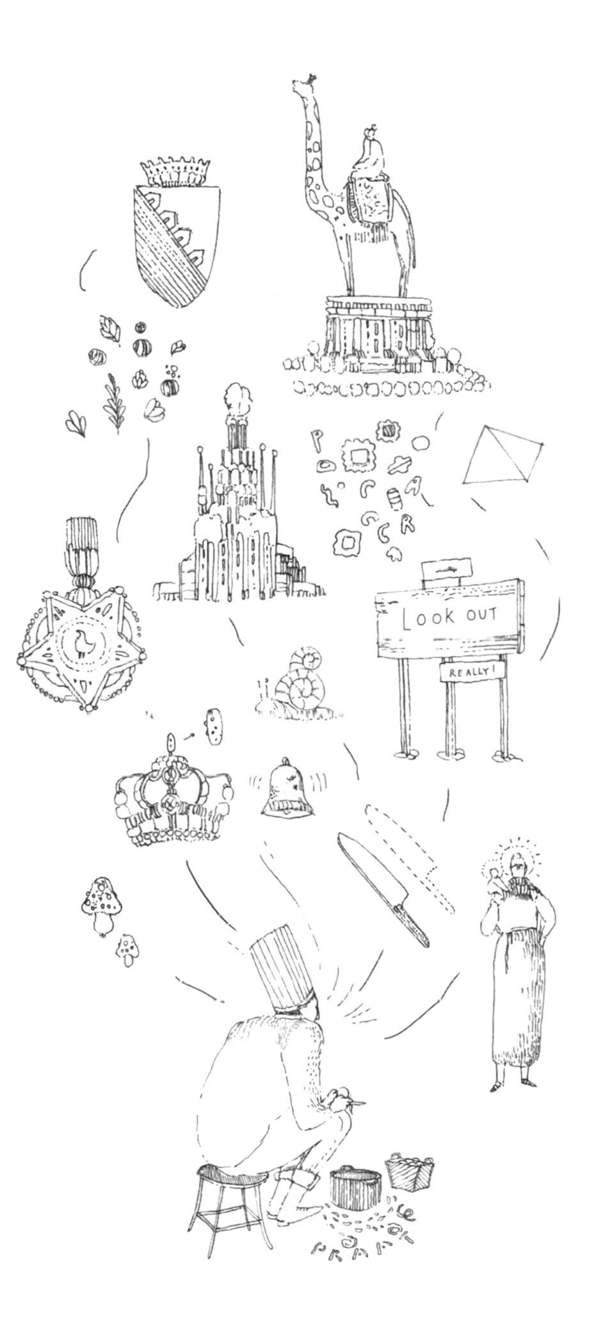

lost and it must be found! Ah, is that the bell ringing for half past three already? Doesn't time fly! Where has that cleaver got to? Blast it!"

He was like an old woman.

And since they had arrived in Blät, Half-George's appetite had vanished too. He had become unable to stomach anything but oatmeal porridge, which he shared with the convent cat.

Tortot gave Half-George the task of making some herbal mixtures for him and putting them in bottles of oil. He had placed an old kitchen table in front of the barrel, with the bottles in alphabetical order.

"All right, then, I'm off out."

Half-George nodded.

"To market, if you're interested."

Tortot left the convent kitchen, locked the door with one of his keys, popped the bunch of keys into his pocket and headed out. At that same moment, the convent cat slipped inside. The mean, suspicious animal, which hissed at everyone and everything, had for some unknown reason made friends with Half-George and liked to sit inside his barrel.

The bell in the tower rang out.

Tok-Bong. Tok-Bong.

The strange sound was the result of the enemy's last attack.

A cannonball had blasted a hole in the quarter bell. Since then, every other swing, the clapper hit the hole instead of the metal.

Grumbling, Tortot led his donkey through the crowded streets. Blät was swarming with soldiers. Anyone who was wealthy or lucky had been billeted in houses. Everyone else had been given permission to use scrap material to build huts and sheds in the alleyways.

The term "scrap material", though, was interpreted loosely. The mayor had his hands full dealing with angry townsfolk who had suddenly found themselves without a front door, washerwomen who had lost their baskets of sheets, and couples who could see the starry sky from their bed at night because half of the roof tiles had been stolen. The city, once so orderly, was looking more and more like one of the bankrupt cities of the East. It was full to bursting with cloths and rags, piled-up bales of straw and ingenious constructions of tiles, planks and clay.

The attacks from Vladzimka had also taken their toll.

The city wall had collapsed in several places, and the impact of the cannonballs had caused the ground around the well to subside, so the water was rationed and the townsfolk had to fetch it in small pewter mugs instead of buckets.

And then there were the disfigured emperors.

Before the War of the Gherkins, Blät had been one of the most fanatical supporters of the Twin Emperors' rule. The city had reached deep into its pockets so that artists could lavish their attention on creating various depictions of the two emperors in all their radiant beauty. The most extravagant project had been a twenty-foot statue called *The Beauty and Wisdom of the Imperial Emperors.*

When the War of the Gherkins broke out, however, this love proved short-lived. The pragmatic city council decided to remove one emperor from every likeness of the two. But there were so many statues that even now, two years later, the job still was not finished.

Even before Tortot saw the sutler, he spotted the Ottovarian halberd leaning against a weathered wall.

It had been more than two years since he had last seen Couraz. Entire cities had burned to the ground, populations had fled, there had been murdering and plundering aplenty, but Tortot had never doubted for a moment that the sutler was still alive. It was not that he had missed her—the very thought!—but, well, there was a certain logic to her presence.

Couraz greeted him with the same indifference as he did her. Her thumbless hand made a vague waving gesture as if she were shooing a fly away.

"See anything to your liking, field cook? I have turnips, celeriac, carrots fresh from the field."

The turnips were as dry as dust, the celeriac was mouldy, and the carrots felt soft and bendy.

That was not her fault, though. Since the city had been shut up tight, food entered only in dribs and drabs.

Sometimes, a convoy of smugglers managed to bring in new supplies, but they were often attacked and robbed. Not by the enemy, but by organized bands of robbers. People had been trying to grow food in the city itself, but with little success: the alleyways were in the shade most of the day and the ground was too stony.

"I'll take everything you've got," said Tortot.

"Fifteen pieces of silver."

"FIFTEEN?"

"Fifteen," repeated Couraz, "and I'll throw in a twist of sugar for free."

She lit a cigarette that was filled with some kind of sugared herb. The intoxicating smoke made Tortot dizzy. They haggled for a while and finally, grumbling contentedly, he paid.

"May Allah give you seven sons," said Couraz automatically, blowing smoke through her nose. The smoke was surprisingly dense. As he leaned closer to her, her eyes flashed bright green, and he said quietly, "I need milk and oatmeal."

The sutler looked at him mockingly. "Anything else? The Holy Grail perhaps? The Shroud of Turin?"

"I thought maybe you..."

"I'm a sutler, field cook, not a miracle worker."

"But somewhere there must be..."

"All the cows have been eaten. The oats are in the enemy's hands."

Surreptitiously, he took out his own money bag. Couraz irritably waved her hand. "Money, money. What good is money these days?"

And when Tortot gave her a puzzled look, she said, "Fine, later, when the war's over. But now? Even at the best inns all I can get is chicken feed."

And then she spoke the name of a world-famous dish from the north, briefly slipping into a foreign accent, short and clipped, which immediately made it clear that (just as Tortot had always suspected) not one drop of Ottovarian blood flowed through her veins.

"Well... can you make it for me?"

Couraz said it casually, but in her eyes he saw a gleam of hidden longing.

"Can you get me milk and oatmeal?" replied Tortot.

She scornfully clicked her tongue. "I'm a sutler. If necessary, I can get hold of the kneecap of the Blessed Virgin."

"But you just said..."

"That was then and this is now, Tortot."

With the sutler's supplies loaded onto his donkey, Tortot hurried to the quarters of the former colonel Nilliewasser, now a general. He found him, as so often recently, studying his books on military strategy, trying to master the latest siege-breaking techniques. He was wearing just a jerkin and the bottom part of his armour. The sweet scent of magnolia lingered heavily around him, but could not entirely conceal another penetrating odour.

"Sapping, entrenchment, circumvallation," Tortot heard him mutter. "But what was the blasted fourth one again?"

"Contravallation," said Tortot.

With an exasperated look the general glanced up, but that annoyance vanished as soon as he saw the field cook. With a sigh of relief, he closed the book.

"Ah, Tortot. Come in, come in! The sergeant will take your coat. Crookleg? Crookleg!"

The sergeant's horsey face peered around the corner.

"Come along! What are you dilly-dallying for? Take his coat!"

With an expression that was somewhere between formal politeness and sheer loathing, Crookleg took Tortot's coat and disappeared again.

"There, that's better. What's on the menu this evening?"

Tortot thought about the marinated rats and the sutler's questionable vegetables.

"Pickled rabbit in wine sauce on a bed of fresh spring ratatouille," he said without batting an eyelid.

"Excellent. I'm sure the senior officers will enjoy that," the general said vaguely.

The Poker Player himself ate very little these days. Even when all the screws and buckles of his armour had been fastened as tightly as possible, he still rattled like a tinsmith's cart.

That was not the only sign that he was a changed man. His beloved poker cards lay unused on the table. The only mirror in the room was covered with a black cloth.

One morning, Nilliewasser the Fair, also known as Fairface, had been found stone-dead on his camp bed, less than twenty miles from Blät. The surgeon put it down to a heart attack.

Fairface was buried in the nearest peasants' graveyard. The intention had been to give him a military salute, but the gunpowder was too damp. In the end, they removed the cannonball from the barrel. Two soldiers carried it ten yards in the pouring rain and laid it down on the earth, to symbolize the major's path through life.

Just as it was unthinkable for a general to spill tears for a major (even if it was his own son), it was unimaginable for a brother to cry for his own brother.

Crookleg buried Fairface with such eagerness that it seemed as if he wanted to escort him to the other side of the earth.

In the days that followed, Crookleg was everywhere and nowhere: he dragged back captured cannons, carried out reckless charges in no-man's-land, volunteered for double night watches, was always the first to roll call and studied his father's textbooks until the general dismissed him with an impatient gesture.

And when the next round of promotions came, he was once again overlooked.

After Tortot had concluded his discussions with the Poker Player about the menu for the coming week and they had made small talk for a while, he took his leave. His donkey was still waiting outside; the big brown eyes behind the lenses had shrunk to the size of coffee beans. He stared at the field cook with an expression that was reproachful yet understanding.

Tortot suddenly felt a pang of love for the animal. What he really wanted to do was wrap his arms around his donkey's neck and give it a hug, but that was quite clearly unthinkable.

Just then, he remembered the twist of sugar.

It was only as he took the sugar from his coat pocket, frowned and then slipped his hand back into his pocket that he discovered the keys to the convent kitchen were gone.

CHAPTER 22

The difference between a cake and a petit four

Half-George had been woken by the sound of the crippled bell. It could not be heard clearly from the cellar, but the walls conducted the vibrations so well that it shook all the way down into the gherkin barrel.

It was a moment before he realized that he had once again been dreaming about the biggest war ever. In the middle of that dream, at the point where the soldiers were aiming the barrel of the Castle Killer at Half-George and his brothers, a strange, blissful sleep took hold of him. His brothers, who were sitting on the highest branches around him, had smiled and said, "Go on. It's been a long day." And within the sleep in that sleep there was another sleep, and then another and another, like the rings of an onion, and the sleep grew deeper and deeper, darker and darker, and more and more peaceful, until Half-George had fallen so deeply that he was very reluctant to wake up.

If he had been less drowsy, maybe he would have heard that the first key that was inserted into the lock did not fit—and neither did the second one. Maybe he would have heard the quiet curse and then the grunt of glee when the final key did turn in the lock. And maybe then Half-George would have recognized the footsteps coming down the stairs.

But all the half-soldier felt was a weary happiness that the field cook had returned. He suddenly regretted having been so quiet and withdrawn in recent days.

"Was it busy, Tortot? Were there lots of market stalls? Maybe you could take me with you one day. Who's going to notice if you have a barrel on the cart? I bet there are plenty of traders with barrels, aren't there?"

The sleepiness had even crept into his voice and his arms felt heavy, so heavy. Half-George was too tired to pull himself upright, but he still made an effort. "We shouldn't wait too long though, eh?" he called from the barrel. "Summer's nearly over, isn't it?"

The footsteps came closer.

"Tortot?"

A shadow fell over the barrel.

In his hurry, Tortot had decided to leave his donkey. He cursed the stream of people, who seemed to exist only to slow him down. He had never understood when soldiers said they could feel their hearts in their mouths or their knees knocking at the start of a battle. What nonsense! A heart belonged in your chest and knees did not really knock.

But this time he felt both. He was short of breath, tripped over, scraped his hands on the stony ground and struggled back to his feet. He heard people laughing and he really would have liked to punch the lot of them, but his legs had taken on a life of their own, seeming years younger, stronger, and he ran onwards, clutching the stitch in his side.

Just as Tortot ran through the arch and into the courtyard, a nun happened to be leaving the convent.

The bewildered nun was just able to step out of the way in time.

"God does not have a closing time, my son," she chided him.

"And neither does the devil," Tortot managed to pant back at her.

Fur on end, the convent cat stood hissing outside the kitchen door, which was slightly ajar. It looked confused when it saw Tortot coming, as it did not know whether to hiss at the door or at him. The field cook impatiently shooed the creature away.

Crookleg had dragged the half-soldier out of his barrel. Half-George was lying on his side. There was a long and bloody scratch from his temple to his cheek.

Tortot had the presence of mind to close the door quietly.

"Ah, Tortot," said Crookleg, without turning around. "Aren't you going to say hello?"

"Leave the boy alone," said Tortot.

"Boy?" said Crookleg. "I could have sworn it was a gherkin. Well, half a gherkin."

He dragged Half-George around a quarter of a turn, so that he could look at Tortot.

"I'm disappointed in you, Tortot," said Crookleg. "I expected you at least to try to act surprised. 'Where on earth did that come from? Was it in the barrel? I had no idea!'"

"Leave the boy alone," said Tortot again.

Crookleg placed his granite heel on the side of Half-George's head. There was no weight resting on it. Not yet. Half-George had closed his eyes. He had turned so white that he was almost translucent.

"I knew it," said Crookleg. "All this time I knew you were up to something. This is going to be a fine execution. Harbouring a deserter. Being a deserter yourself. At least I assume you'll admit it now."

He applied a minimal amount of pressure to the heel. Half-George groaned.

"Of course," said Tortot quickly.

"Such a shame a person can only die once."

It was not as if Tortot had a plan at that moment, and if he did have anything remotely resembling a plan it was veiled in a mist that was lifting painfully slowly. But he went with his own words. Because they were all he had.

"Do you know what I think of when I see you?" said Tortot.

"Sorry?"

"Of a man standing in front of a baker's shop window, gazing at the tiny little petits fours, because he thinks he'll never be able to have the great big cake that's next to them."

"Sorry?"

"You think too modestly for a man of your stature."

Crookleg's eyes darted back and forth, as if he could not decide whether to feel insulted or flattered.

"Fine," said Tortot. "You've caught two deserters. That's not much in the grand scheme of things. A tiny little petit four with a teeny dollop of whipped cream! With a bit of luck, your father will be in a good mood and he'll promote you to junior officer. All right, let's say he's in a particularly good mood and he makes you a major. But does that do any justice to your boundless ambition, your dazzling expertise? Could you not surpass your brother—no, your father—with ease? Is that not, in fact, your duty? So..."

Tortot fell silent. He sat down on the stairs and studied his nails. Then he tapped one finger on his lip and gazed dreamily at the ceiling. He seemed to have completely forgotten both Nilliewasser and Half-George.

"So?..." echoed Crookleg.

Tortot looked up, irritated. "Just stop it."

“What?”

“You are an outstanding military man, with more talent in one finger than that whole bunch of officers and generals put together, but you’re no actor. You know very well what I’m getting at.”

“Of course I do,” said Crookleg, who did not have the faintest idea.

“Alexander the Great? Julius Caesar?”

“Um...”

“Do you think they ever thought: ‘Oh, I’ll just have a biscuit’?”

“If you’re imagining you can butter me up, you’re very much mistaken,” said Crookleg, now quite clearly flattered. “And don’t go thinking you can avoid your punishment.”

“Ah, punishment. It’s no big deal,” said Tortot. “I’ve been living on borrowed time ever since the moment you worked out what was going on. You had me figured out straight away. You were the only one. I’ve been a dead man walking ever since then.”

The sergeant may not have been the brightest of men, but he had enough common sense to realize that Tortot’s argument was heading somewhere. He scented some kind of promise in the air, although he had no idea what that promise might be. To be quite honest, neither did Tortot. All he knew was that the carrot

he dangled in front of Crookleg's nose had to be so big and juicy that it made the sergeant dizzy with longing.

He was shocked himself when he came up with the idea, but there was no turning back. "It's about time you received what you are entitled to."

"What?"

The sergeant's mouth was slightly open. Like a hungry wood oven.

Tortot turned around and hung his coat on the hook beside the door. He did it very precisely; the hanging loop was a little twisted and he straightened it out, smoothing it between his thumb and forefinger as if this were the most important act of his entire life. In a sense, that was true. And as he did so, he said casually, "What? The invasion and capture of Vladzimka, of course. By you personally."

CHAPTER 23

In which the exceedingly brilliant master chef carries out his plan

After Crookleg left, Half-George was shaking so badly that Tortot had to put the tea cosy on his head to stop it banging against the side of the barrel. And the most ridiculous thing was that it seemed to be contagious—his own hands were shaking too.

The half-soldier still said nothing, did nothing. Not when Tortot lit the oven, not when he had a big pot simmering away above the fire and a sweet and spicy scent filled the kitchen.

It was only when Tortot had transferred the stew and the vegetable casserole into two big jars with lids, wrapped cloths around the jars and lowered them into a sack, packed them in with straw, and then put on his coat that Half-George finally seemed to wake up.

"What are you doing?"

"Nothing."

"Where are you going?"

"Nowhere."

"Tortot?" He heard the panic in Half-George's voice.

Tortot turned around. He walked over to the barrel. Patted the half-soldier's bony shoulder. "I'll be back."

He picked up the lantern, lit it and headed outside.

Couraz lived in Blät's former aviary. Most of the goldfinches, siskins and canaries had died of fright when the War of the Gherkins broke out. Not even the peacock (the heraldic symbol of Blät) had survived, but there was a more

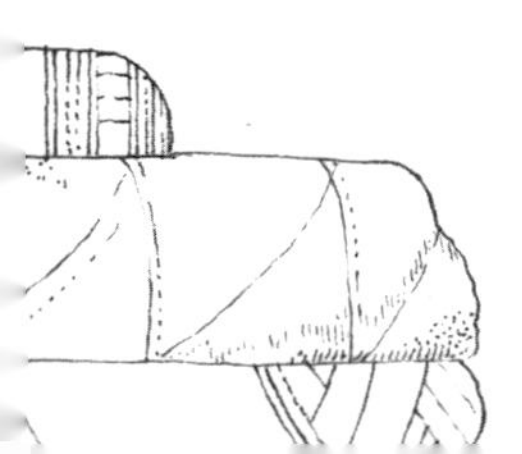

practical reason for that. Some of the citizens of Blät felt so guilty that they still heard the bird's angry cries every night. And they had not even enjoyed the peacock that much. It had been like eating cork.

Couraz had made the aviary a comfortable place. Cloths printed with attractive designs hung from the ceiling, dividing the space in three, a carpet lay on the floor, and she had decorated a few sacks and arranged them in the corner

as cushions. Sheets of rice paper were pegged on a clothesline, occasionally rustling in the draught.

Tortot saw that many of her belongings were packed and stacked in one corner. Otherwise, the room was empty.

The milk and oatmeal were waiting for him.

"Welcome," said the sutler, her eyes fixed on the sack the field cook was holding.

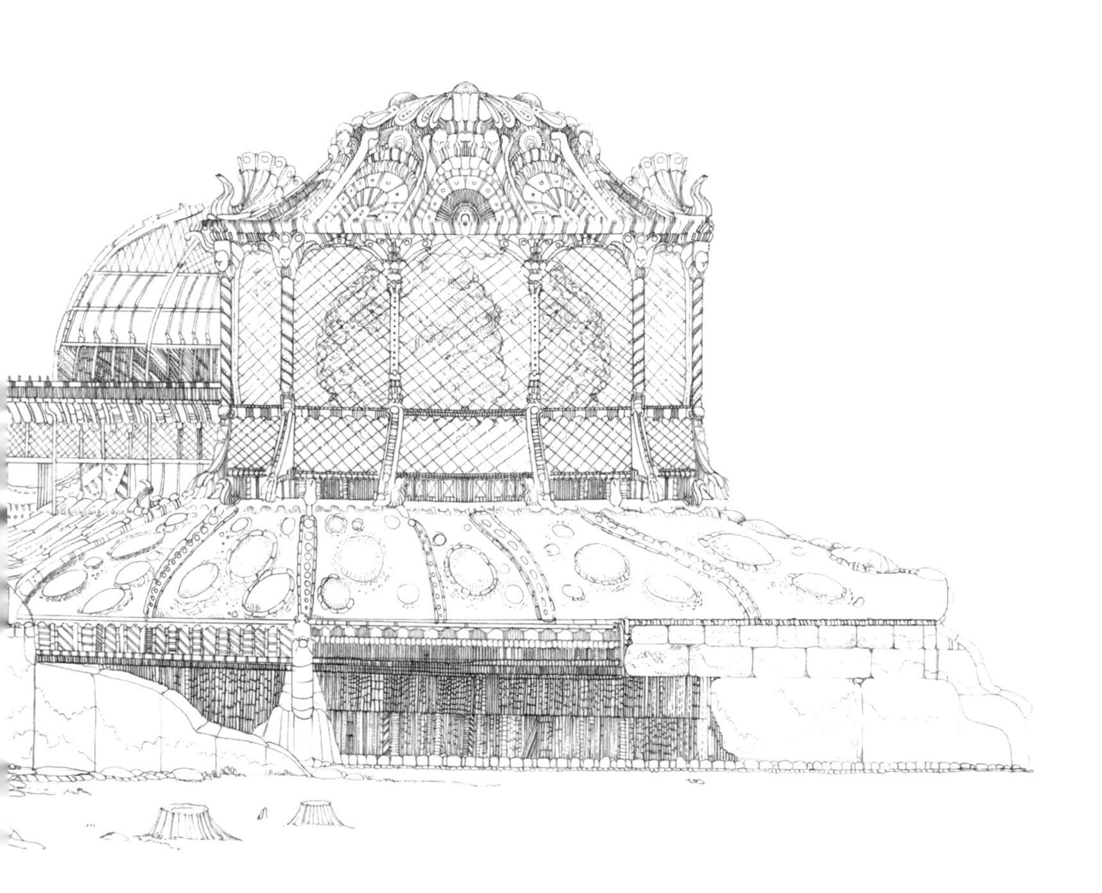

He served up the dish. As the delicious scent steamed from the plate, the sutler's eyes opened wide for a moment. As if she were inhaling it with her eyes.

She ate calmly but, as Tortot knew, greed is impossible to hide. For some people, it was a trembling eyelid that gave them away, others swung one leg, and Tortot had once known an admiral who suffered from double hiccoughs whenever he ate pears stewed in cinnamon liqueur.

For Couraz, it was the tendons of her forearm. They were so taut that you could have played the lute on them.

"I bet you sometimes get tired of this city," said Tortot.

Couraz looked at him.

"Well, if all the oatmeal is in the hands of Vladzimka, and you can still conjure up oatmeal, then..."

"Then?"

"Then you must know of a secret entrance. And once you're in Vladzimka, then you must overhear a thing or two, mustn't you?"

Couraz did not bat an eyelid, but Tortot knew what homesickness could do to a person.

And the sutler, even though she was a veteran of war, was no exception. He held the two jars under her nose. "Another helping?"

With the right food, you could get anyone to talk. And it was not long before Tortot had found out enough to be extremely concerned.

"A shipment of lettuce has arrived in Vladzimka," Tortot said that afternoon.

"Lettuce? Lettuce? What good is lettuce to me?" grumbled Crookleg. "Tell me something useful!"

They were in the stables. The sergeant had been ordered to supervise a group of hussars who were mucking out. It had not gone very well. Somehow a fresh load of horse dung had ended up on Crookleg's expensive boots. He was still furiously polishing away when Tortot found him. Ducklings scampered about his feet, searching for bugs in the straw.

"Well," said Tortot quietly. "I thought you might be interested to hear that the lettuce was escorted by a regiment of three hundred and fifty soldiers disguised as peasants."

The stains on the sergeant's boots were growing larger and filthier. He was so annoyed by now that he took his musket and fired at the hussars. Most of the horses were exhausted and barely looked up, but one of the ducklings was so frightened that it deposited a tiny dropping, and the hussars scrambled about frantically, buzzing around like a swarm of mosquitoes.

"Ox gall," said Tortot.

"What?"

"Ox gall. That'll remove every stain."

The sergeant shouted for ox gall and the soldiers ran out of the stables.

"And of course you realize that a whole regiment is a little extreme," said Tortot. "Even with bands of robbers in the area."

"What do you mean?"

"That one might wonder exactly what's so special about these provisions that each individual lettuce needs its own personal guard..."

"Eh?..."

Tortot pictured the interior of Crookleg's head as an extremely simple machine with only two cogs, but even then they still both managed to turn the wrong way.

"Could it be that the imperial provisions have arrived?" said Tortot.

Couraz had been sure of it. The balance of power that had lasted for months was over. Seven counties that had been allied with Blät had unexpectedly sided with the enemy emperor.

"But why on earth would they do that?" Tortot had asked.

Couraz shrugged. "Who knows? Maybe they want to break the deadlock. This war is devouring soldiers and equipment. But maybe they just got bored."

Whatever the case, this shift of power had not worked out in Blät's favour.

When Tortot heard the news, he suddenly understood why all Couraz's belongings were packed. And why she had hardly any new stock.

"The question is not *whether* Blät will fall," Tortot explained to Crookleg, "but *when*—and at what cost. The seven counties have sent troops, and the enemy emperor is so sure of victory that he has come incognito to Vladzimka. He wants to see Blät fall with his own eyes."

Tortot had always viewed the sergeant as a raging bull: brute force, but easily led up the garden path. A red rag here, a meadow of clover there—and Bob was your uncle.

But the icy calm that suddenly descended upon Crookleg made Tortot wonder if he had misjudged him.

"Aha," said the sergeant.

"Aha?"

"Then I'm curious."

"What about?"

"This masterplan of yours."

"Ah, yes."

"At least I'm assuming you have a masterplan, don't you?"

"Of course," replied Tortot.

"Excellent."

"I just need to polish the final details."

"Sounds good."

"It is."

"Because it would be a shame if you hadn't worked it out yet. A shame for you and your little soldier friend." And then, without blinking, he changed the subject and asked: "Does ox gall really remove every stain?"

The sergeant shifted his weight and raised his boot. The ducklings were still running around his feet. It was yet another hot day. The little creatures were clearly feeling the heat, particularly the smallest one, which was panting, its tiny tongue hanging out of its beak. The granite heel of the boot cast a cool and tempting shadow on the straw. The duckling looked up, its beady little black eyes gleaming.

A shadow no larger than a lady's handkerchief.

Ducklings don't ask for much.

The movement was calm, controlled and surprisingly quick. Then Crookleg wiped his heel on the straw.

"I want your plan by the day after tomorrow at the latest," he said as he left. "Or the fun will soon be over for you and your half-friend."

CHAPTER 24

The emperor's nose

There were no more dreams. Firstly, Tortot hardly slept. And when he did sleep, it was as if someone had suddenly pulled a sack over his head. There were no images, no sounds, no smells. There was only a terrible sense of longing, but he barely knew what for.

The boy, though, dreamed enough for two.

"It's not true!" he called out in the middle of the night. "It's not true."

Putting chili peppers in his ears did not help. Half-George continued to rave and ramble, the cold sweat pouring from his forehead. Tortot tried to shake him awake, but it was not easy.

By the time he had finally managed to hoist the shivering lad out of his barrel, Tortot was so covered in sweat himself that he almost slid over on his slippery feet.

Luckily, Half-George was awake by then. But the dream was still in his head.

"It's a lie!"

"What?"

"Fish *do* cry! They do!"

"Fish? What's all this about fish?"

"I've seen it myself! They cry at night, Tortot."

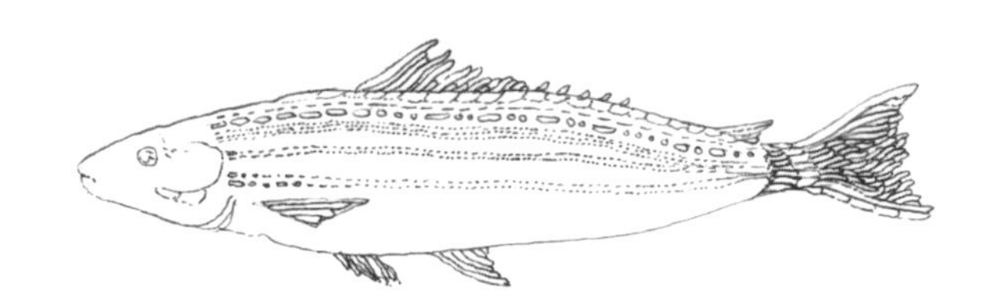

"Yes, yes. Hush now."

"That's why the sea is salty. They've filled the sea with their tears. With their tears, Tortot! Their tears!"

"It's all right, lad. Shh."

"No, you don't understand!"

"I do understand. I really do."

"You don't. You DON'T!"

"The sea is salty," said Tortot, rocking Half-George. "And the fish have filled the sea. With their tears. You see, I do get it. Do you see?"

He repeated the sentences over and over, like a lullaby. Until Half-George drifted off to sleep.

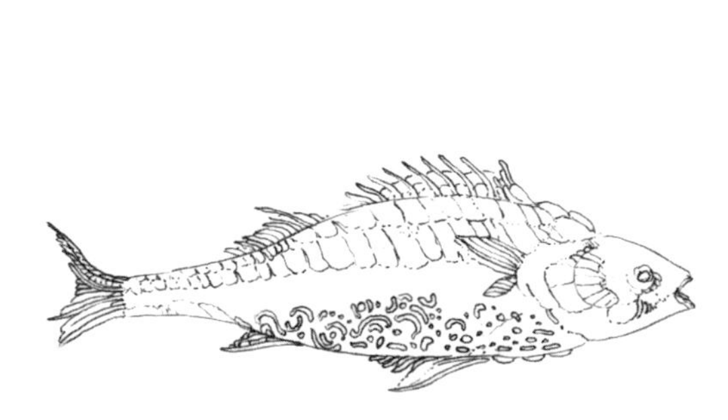

That night, Tortot wandered through the city on his donkey. There was a full moon. In spite of the warm night, the streets were quiet. Even the most persistent troublemakers and hoodlums were lying exhausted in their shelters made of canvas and bales of straw. At the Red House, a couple of ladies of pleasure were leaning out of the windows, murmuring quietly to one another. When they saw Tortot they waved mechanically, but then, without waiting for a response, went straight back to the tarot cards that were laid out on the window ledge.

Negotiating the narrow streets with the donkey was tricky, but Tortot had saddled it without thinking. He was happy to have the animal to keep him company, even though it was tiring, as he had forgotten to put the donkey's spectacles on.

As a result, the donkey mistook moon shadows for obstacles and overlooked actual obstacles, and so Tortot nearly went tumbling from his saddle twice. The donkey seemed jumpy. Was the creature getting old? Had it really been that young when he bought it?

He tried to remember, but his mind was foggy.

When the donkey prepared to jump over the shadow of a cart, its legs shaking with anticipation, Tortot decided to dismount.

Walking is good for thinking.

Half-George had to get out of this war.

Tortot had known that for a long time now, but it had never been quite so clear before.

Yes, he had to get out of this war, and soon.

If that had been the only problem, it would have been tricky enough. But somehow Tortot had managed to saddle himself with a number of other challenges. What was this plan he had dangled in front of Crookleg? How on earth was he going to make sure the sergeant captured Vladzimka? He had tried to pry information out of Couraz about the secret entrance to the city. And did she happen to have a map of the citadel, or something along those lines?...

"Do you think I'm tired of life?" she had said. "What do you think? How long will it take them to find out who revealed the secret entrance? Or who the map belongs to?"

"But by then we'll have conquered Vladzimka and it won't matter, will it? Then you'll have done a great service to Blät."

"Ah, but the question is, will it work?" replied Couraz. "And even if it Blät does win, I'd still be risking my life. It wouldn't be the first time an informer was executed for being a double agent. No, thank you."

All she would say was that the citadel of Vladzimka was an insane labyrinth and that there was little point trying to find the way on your own. Besides, the secret entrance could only be opened from the inside, using a complex system of hidden keys.

"And I've already told you more than I'd like," said the sutler.

There was something else that was troubling Tortot.

It was an unexpected offer that Couraz had made.

"Come with me, Tortot. With your talent as a cook and my talent at conjuring up any provisions you might need, we'd make the perfect team. Just imagine: a sutler and a cook. If we work together, we could make a fortune on any battlefield. No more market stall selling products for a field cook to turn into dishes, but ready-made meals instead. A travelling restaurant. It could be a goldmine."

But she had made her feelings about the boy perfectly clear. He was not sure why he had told her about him. Maybe the beer she had poured was stronger than it looked.

"Three wheels make a crooked cart," she had said. "And I don't know where he's from, what his history is."

"He's a boy, practically a child," said Tortot.

"In a war, there are only soldiers," Couraz replied firmly. "And I can't run the risk of being arrested again. I didn't enjoy it the last time." She instinctively clutched the hand that was missing a thumb. "Think about it, cook, but not for too long. It'll be less than a week before Blät falls, and I don't want to be here when that happens."

It would be so easy. Tortot had drifted for long enough. For too long.

He had not realized, though; it was the sutler who had opened his eyes. He had no illusions about the partnership that Couraz had mentioned. She certainly had no need for any romantic fuss and nonsense. And neither had he, and he had no idea why. Never had had.

The strange feeling of butterflies that was stopping him from sleeping had less to do with Couraz herself or with the dream she had presented to him. No, this was about his own dream. A dream so secret and hidden that he had not even known he had it until Couraz had made her offer.

A restaurant at the end of the world.

A restaurant beyond the war.

He could picture the place so clearly that the streets and alleyways took on the form of a kitchen, a small café beneath grapevines, basic wooden tables.

It would be so simple.

And he was tired.

Tired of looking after the child.

He told himself that he had done more than anyone could have expected of him.

The boy was not his son; he did not belong to him. Tortot was not the one who had made the child, and he was not the one who had broken him. The boy was not his responsibility.

Couraz was right: Three wheels make a crooked cart.

For five minutes, he held on to the dream; for five minutes, he felt blissfully happy and filled with relief; for five minutes, he came up with menus, table arrangements, damask tablecloths, silver cutlery and names for his restaurant. Then it was all swept away by an unstoppable wave of realization.

He was indeed a fish. Not a stingray at the bottom of the ocean, not ice-cold and calculating, but the brainless kind that mistook a hook for a worm.

From the moment Half-George had popped his head out of the gherkin barrel and asked if he was past the war—no, even before that—from the moment the young soldier had walked into Tortot's life, when he was still a whole George, wearing his brother's chamois-leather boots, a line had been cast.

And Tortot had taken the bait, without even knowing he was biting.

For just one moment, he hated the lad so much that it shocked him.

And, when it dawned on him what that hatred really meant, he was even more shocked.

At first light, by which time Tortot was more or less sleepwalking and was not a jot closer to solving a single one of his problems, his donkey dashed past him in a burst of enthusiasm, banging its head for the thirty-fourth time that night. This time it was against *The Beauty and Wisdom of the Imperial Emperors*. Panicked voices came from the other side of the statue.

"Look what you've gone and done!"

"What I've done? You're the one holding the chisel!"

"The chisel you gave me! Because you didn't dare!"

Four sculptors had spent five years working on the enormous statue. One of the emperors had been sitting on a throne with both hands on the armrests and the Book of Wisdom on his lap. The other emperor had stood beside him with his right arm over the headrest of his brother's throne. In his hand he had held the Apple of Virtue.

When Tortot walked around to the other side, he saw that the restoration was not going well. All that was left of the standing emperor was the arm over the headrest, and the seated emperor had lost his left arm, so that it looked as if the remaining emperor had, for some unknown reason, deposited his own left arm on the headrest behind him.

But that was not the worst of it.

The chisel must have slipped during an attempt to remove the arm.

"It's your fault!"

"No, it's your fault!"

The tip of the seated emperor's nose lay in pieces on the ground. One of the soldiers started crying. The other picked up a piece of nose and held it aloft, as if hoping the stone emperor would take the tip and reattach it to his nose.

Tortot just stared. Wasn't this absurd? Blät was about to be crushed by the armies of seven counties. The city would be burned, looted, ruined, and the only thing that appeared to worry those in charge was the emperor's vanity. But with good reason. It would not have been the first time a city had been torched because of a wart on a man's face.

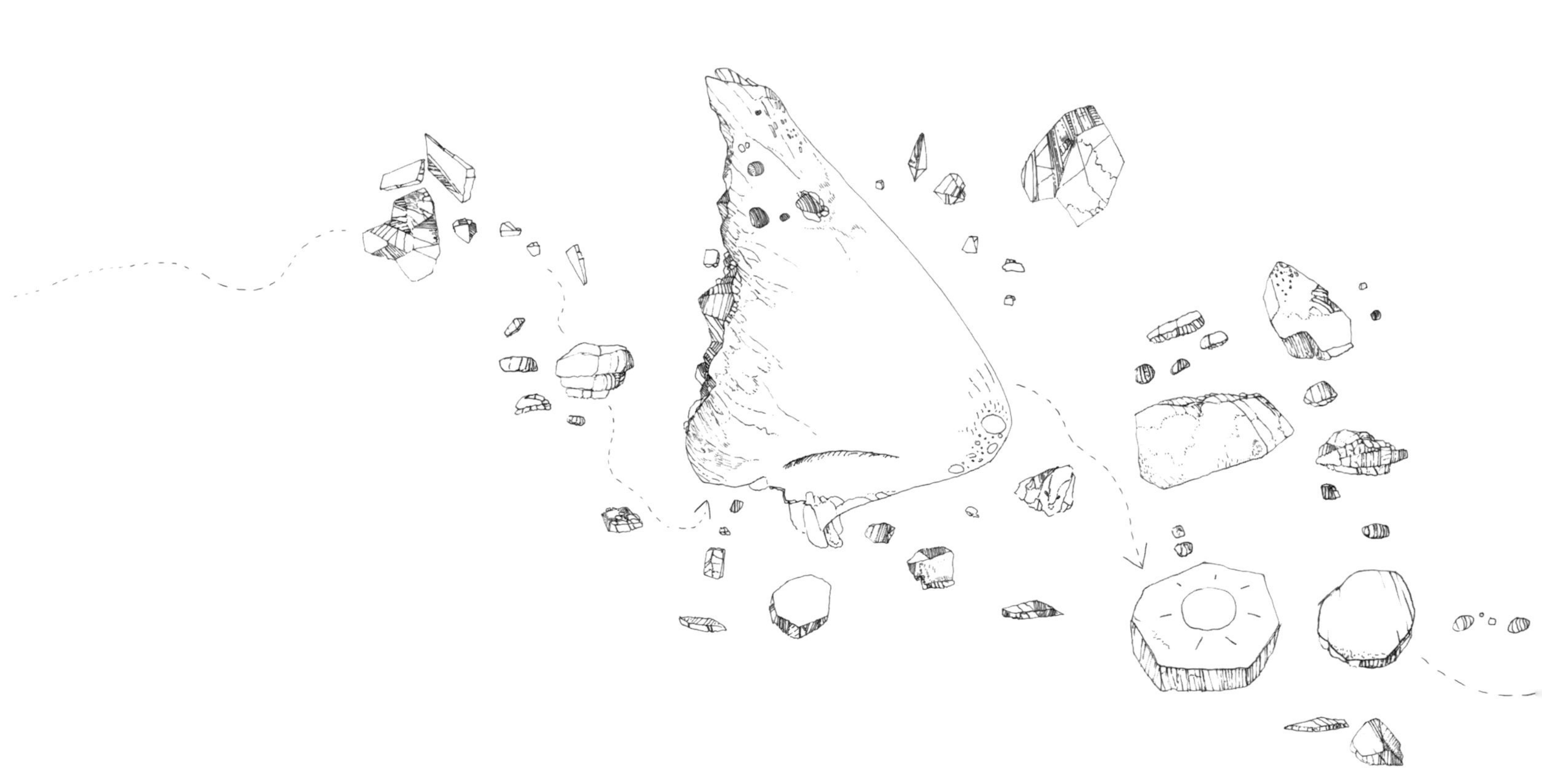

No matter who won, if the victorious emperor saw just one disfigured face as he made his way through the city, a worse fate than any war awaited Blät.

Tortot began to turn heel. His head was tired, his feet hurt, and the air was unpleasantly sultry, which made him long for a refreshing rain shower. But halfway through his turn, he paused.

He looked again at the young hussar, who was still holding up the tip of the nose, like an offering.

The donkey gently nipped Tortot's calf. It wanted to get back to its stable, but Tortot barely even noticed.

A plan was slowly surfacing in his head.

An insane plan, a plan full of enormous risks.

But still: a plan.

dulcis est victoria

CHAPTER 25

Victory is sweet

"I'm sorry," said Crookleg, "I must be getting hard of hearing, but did you say cake?"

Tortot nodded.

"And what are we going to do with that?" sneered the sergeant. "Pelt the enemy to death?"

"We're going to give it away."

"And why is that?"

"As a sign of surrender."

Tortot had worked on the cake for two whole days. It was three tiers high. The top tier had a portrait of the emperor. The pink-marzipan imperial face was as smooth and perfect as a starched sheet. The cheeks blushed with cherry juice, and the eyes, made of blue boiled sweets, sparkled vividly. Tortot had grated the darkest chocolate to make eyebrows and lashes. The slightly parted lips were strawberry jelly, and the teeth were peppermint cream. The emperor's wig was candyfloss, with every lock ending in a perfect curl.

The middle tier was iced with the following words: *dulcis est victoria*. "Victory is sweet."

Of course there was no lack of gherkins, which were arranged all around the emperor as a decorative border on the bottom tier. They were made of mashed sweet beans and coloured with nettle juice.

Couraz had spent three days tracking down all the ingredients. It was nothing short of a miracle. When Tortot went to pay her, she had snapped, "Away with you! I don't need money for everything."

And then she had given him something.

"What is it?" he had asked.

"What is what?"

"What you just put in my hands."

She raised an eyebrow. "I didn't put anything in your hands."

Crookleg stared at him. "We're giving them a cake?"

Tortot nodded.

"That's your plan? Your masterplan?"

"Yes."

"This is just a question," said Crookleg. "Probably a stupid one, I'll admit. But how is giving them a cake going to help me to capture Vladzimka?"

Then he frowned and looked at Tortot. "It's a hollow cake?"

Tortot nodded.

The sergeant looked decidedly disgruntled. "Every idiot knows the story of Troy. No city would be so foolish as to allow in a cake with an army hidden inside."

"The cake's not big enough for that."

"So it's a poisonous cake, then. And why would they be stupid enough to allow a cake from their enemies into the city?"

"They don't have to be stupid, just scared," said Tortot. "And to clear up any doubts: the cake is not poisonous."

And he explained his plan.

Crookleg's expression was sceptical at first, then incredulous and, finally, completely flabbergasted.

When the Poker Player heard about the plan, he steepled his fingers, rested his wrinkled, emaciated head on the tips of those fingers and stared first at Tortot and then at Crookleg, with a blank expression on his face.

If Tortot had not loathed Crookleg, he would have felt sorry for him. The sergeant so clearly longed for his father's approval that it was almost painful.

"And this is your plan, son?" asked the Poker Player. But he was not looking at Crookleg. His gaze was fixed on Tortot.

"Yes," said Tortot. "It's his plan."

A sudden commotion came from the street. When the Poker Player opened the curtain, they saw a bunch of townsfolk fighting over a market vendor's last wares. A carrot rolled across the ground and four people dived on it.

It took ten soldiers to restore order.

The Poker Player sighed. "Fine."

"You think it's a good plan?" said Crookleg, beaming.

"I think it's a completely crackpot plan," said the Poker Player. "But given the situation, we have little choice."

"Listen, Half-George," said Tortot quietly. "I have to go away. For a day and a night. If everything goes as planned, I'll be back tomorrow. There's milk and oatmeal porridge for you in the icebox. Just keep a low profile."

He heard Half-George moving inside the barrel.

"Got it?"

Half-George did not reply, but the alert silence within the barrel told Tortot that the boy had heard.

The hollow section of the cake was at the bottom: a wooden cocoon, accessible via a hatch concealed behind a thick layer of marzipan. Crookleg and Tortot both had to kneel down and hold their breath, and even then it felt as if they were about to burst out of the cake.

"Well, it wasn't made for two," said Tortot, trying to avoid the sergeant's rapier, which kept jabbing into his side.

"You must have thought I was crazy," growled the sergeant. "Me alone in that thing? The moment I turned my back, you'd scarper with that little soldier friend of yours. Besides, if this all goes wrong, I want to make certain you lose your head as well."

He leaned against the wooden frame, which gave a worrying creak.

The wood he had used to make the frame was scrap material, as he had not been able to find anything stronger in the plundered streets of Blät. Tortot tried not to think too hard about the hundreds of gallons of cream, custard and jelly above him.

CHAPTER 26

In which the emperor is about to melt

It was early in the morning, so early that the sun had not yet risen, as Tortot's cake passed through the gates of Blät, escorted by a dozen cavalrymen.

Carrying torches and a white flag, the small patrol proceeded along the road to Vladzimka, which was strewn with skulls.

The wheels of the cart were covered with sheep's wool to ease the worst of the bumps, but Tortot still felt as if his kidneys were in his ears and his eyes were about to bounce out of his head. Judging by Crookleg's grumbling, the sergeant was not doing much better.

As they approached the walled citadel of Vladzimka, an alarm sounded. By that time, the sun was just coming up.

"Good God," muttered the sergeant. "I'm already sweating. I hope they don't keep us waiting outside the gate for too long."

"I don't think they will," replied Tortot.

They heard the guards walking back and forth along the wall. The cake was so close that they could make out every word.

"What's that?"

"You can see what it is, can't you?"

"I can see that I can see it, but can you see it too?"

Tortot recognized their voices immediately. He felt a huge sense of relief that the two brothers who had once stood guard by the marsh had not gone to meet their maker when they shot each other. But then he pulled himself together. He was getting more and more like an old woman.

"What kind of crazy fool would send a cake?"
"It's got the emperor on it."
"They're surrendering. Look, white flags!"
"It's a trick."
"There must be a bomb inside. Or poison."
"Let's just leave it out there."

Crookleg was grinding his teeth so loudly that it sounded as if the cake were ripping apart. "I told you," he growled. "They're never going to fall for it."

"Be patient," Tortot replied quietly, dabbing his sweaty forehead with his handkerchief.

It was the hottest summer in a hundred years. It was already the end of August, but there seemed no end to it. Quite the opposite, in fact; the day that was dawning promised to be hotter than all the days that had gone before. The sky was a milky blue, full of the dust that no rain showers had washed away. And as the sun began its climb, it grew hotter by the minute.

Tortot knew this was the big moment. His plan relied on three factors: the sun's strength, the emperor's vanity, and everyone else's fear of the emperor.

They heard the guards chuckling.
"Let's just leave it there."
"So it can melt away in the sun."
"And when it rains, it'll wash away."
"And when the wind blows..."
There was a sudden startled silence.
"Do you know what's just occurred to me?"
"No. What's just occurred to you?"
"If we leave the cake outside..."
"Yes?"

"Isn't that the same as leaving the emperor outside?"
"Ooh, blimey..."
"And if it melts... then aren't we actually letting the emperor melt?"

It was the greatest of misconceptions, thought Tortot, that military triumph was the result of clever decisions, tactical insight and great courage on the part of the victors. The opposite was true. Wars were won mainly because of stupidity, ignorance and fear on the part of the losers.

The next thing he knew, the cake was being pushed into Vladzimka.

"*Step one*," whispered Tortot.

As soon as the cake arrived in the courtyard, it was encircled by fourteen hussars.

"Enemy object surrounded, lieutenant. Awaiting orders."

"Um..."

"Should we slash the cake with our swords?"

"Um..."

"Or should we shoot the cake?"

"Maybe we should wait a moment."

"Lieutenant?"

"If we slash the cake with our swords, it's not just the cake we'll be slashing."

"You mean..."

"We'll be slashing our emperor too."

"So shall we shoot it, then?"

"Use your brain, you great lout! What do you think the emperor will say when he sees we've riddled his face with bullets?"

"But, lieutenant! We can't leave the cake standing out in the courtyard either. It'll melt just as quickly here. And a pigeon could fly past at any moment and poo all over the emperor!"

Step two, thought Tortot, as the soldiers pushed the cake into the castle of Vladzimka. He could hear them bickering about the best place to put the cake. They finally chose the library, the only room with double doors that were big enough to let the cake through.

Guarding a cake is not the most exciting of activities for a soldier. And as it smelled so delicious that the soldiers' mouths started to water, and as they were terrified that, sooner or later, they would give in to temptation, they agreed to work in shifts of two soldiers at a time. Unfortunately for Vladzimka, two of those guards were the brothers from the wall. And they already had a fourteen-hour shift behind them.

After seven hours inside the cake, Tortot felt as if his whole body had been put through the wringer. He could not feel his legs anymore. They were not just asleep—they were in a coma. His knees had seized up and every single one of his vertebrae was thumping and throbbing away like an ulcer. Crookleg was not faring much better.

The sergeant was sitting at an awkward angle to take the pressure off his back. ("Don't lean on the frame," said Tortot quietly, when the wood began to creak.) And even though it was considerably cooler within the walls of the castle, the air inside the cake was still stifling. There was such a strong smell of sweat that Tortot was afraid it would overpower the sweet scent of the cake and give them away.

It was another half an hour before he heard a hearty snoring ringing out in duplicate.

The longest half an hour in the field cook's life.

"Now," said Tortot quietly.

To his surprise, Crookleg did not move.

"Sergeant?"

"You go."

"Sorry?"

"You go and look for the keys."

For a moment, Tortot thought the heat must have gone to the sergeant's head. "But that's not what we planned, is it?" he said quietly.

"The cake was going to get us inside. Then we both grab the keys, open the secret entrance and the soldiers of Blät capture the castle."

"I'm staying here."

"Here? Inside the cake? Why?"

"I'm waiting for the big prize."

Looking back, Tortot had to admit that, while Crookleg was perhaps not the brightest light in military history and had inherited little or no tactical awareness from his great-grandfather, he sometimes displayed a surprising amount of common sense when it came to seizing opportunities that presented themselves.

Of course!

In the morning, the emperor would receive the cake.

The sergeant had raised his ambitions. He was not going for the biscuit, or for the petit four, and not even for the cake itself. No, he was going for the entire cake shop. What would gain more respect from his father than if he, Nilliewasser the Crookleg, great-grandson of Nilliewasser the Chicken King, grandson of Nilliewasser the Crushed, and son of Nilliewasser the Poker Player, could in one stroke wipe out the entire family history of blunders, accidents and undeserved victories? If he could single-handedly take the enemy emperor hostage and turn the tide of the war?

"You want to stay inside the cake all night?"

Crookleg did not reply.

Tortot did not think for long. He opened the hatch, wormed his way out and closed the cake behind him. He had to stand and wait for a few minutes until the feeling came back to his limbs.

Meanwhile, the guards sat slumped against the bookshelves, their heads together, as if they had fused into one. Tortot crept past them and took out the stack of rice-paper maps that Couraz had slipped into his hands two nights before.

He still felt weak with relief. This had been the only weakness in his original plan. How he was going to get into the fortress was straightforward enough. But how was he going to find the keys to the secret exit?

"They're all in the right order," Couraz had explained. "Every sheet contains part of the route you'll have to follow. When you've completed a section, just swallow the map. That way, no one will ever be able to work out who helped you."

The maps made it clear that the layout of the castle was complex, to put it mildly. The sheets of rice paper were packed with minute details and they all looked the same; the intricate lines were enough to give anyone a headache.

Tortot soon realized that either some architectural genius with a fondness for labyrinths was behind the design, or that no architect had been involved and they had simply started building at random. Whatever the case, without the rice-paper maps Tortot would have lost his way in no time.

There were no guards. "The entire castle is full of guards, except for the rooms of the emperor himself," Couraz had told him, "because he doesn't want people getting under his feet all the time. And as there's only one entrance to his rooms, he doesn't actually need any guards in there."

And so Tortot wandered from corridor to corridor, from mirror room to grand salon.

Whenever he completed a section of the map, he swallowed it, as promised.

There were four keys. The first key led to the second key, the second to the third and the third to the fourth. The last one would open up the secret corridor that led out of Vladzimka.

It all went so smoothly that it was almost boring. There was not even the slightest obstacle or obstruction, the maps were clear; it felt like a pleasant stroll through the emperor's rooms.

He found the first key hanging behind an enormous tapestry featuring a cityscape of Vladzimka. The second was on the collar of a wolfhound which had a room all of its own and seemed reluctant to give up the key, but Tortot had come prepared and took out a small, hard sausage.

He had just eaten the last-but-four sheet of rice paper when a terrible shriek cut through him and everything started to go wrong.

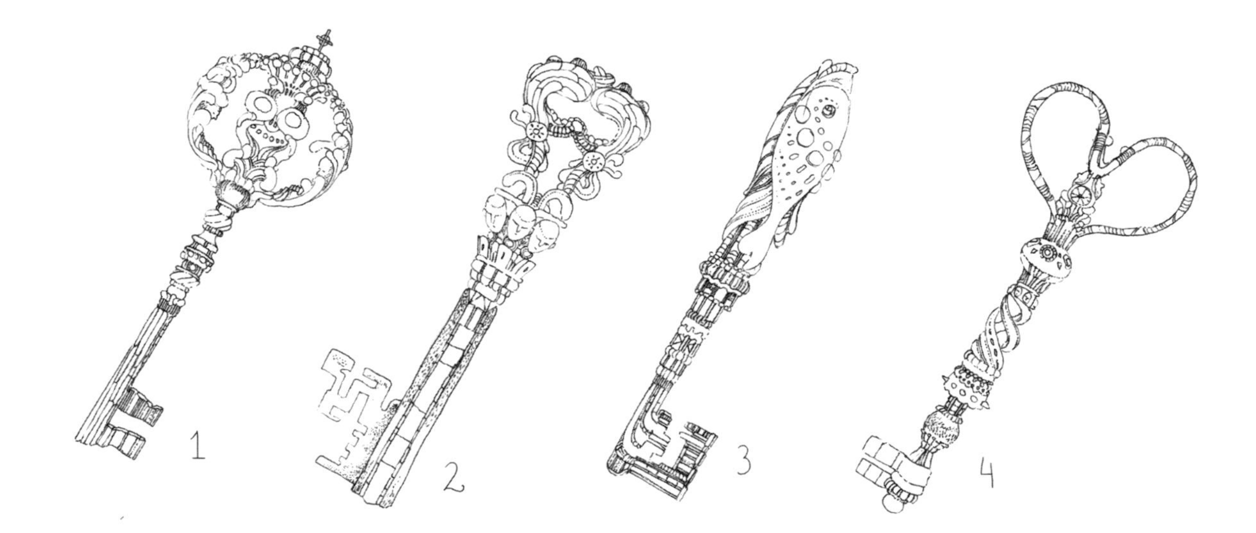

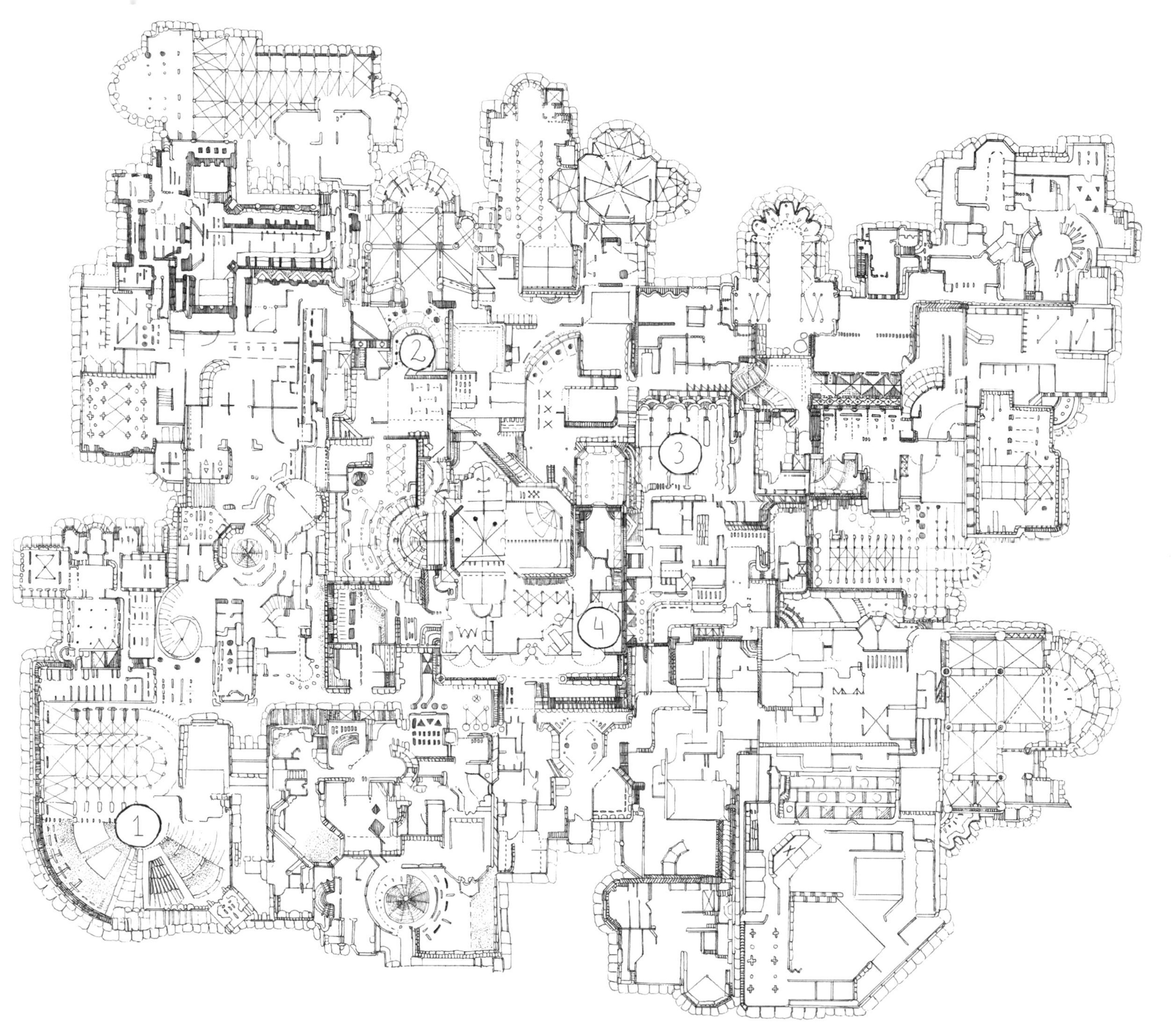
1
2
3
4

CHAPTER 27

In which the emperor cannot sleep

The emperor could not sleep. At the beginning of the heatwave that had plagued the region for a week now, the castle's thick walls had kept the heat at bay, but that night it was seeping through the bricks like hot, thick porridge. As the emperor had no access to his big oak tub in Vladzimka, he ordered his men to fetch big buckets full of gherkin water from the cellars. He was sitting with his backside in one bucket, his feet in two others and dangling his arms in two large pots, but cool relief did not come, and neither did sleep.

The emperor stared at the crooked, chalky-white legs in front of him. He knew that what he saw was not real, that he was cursed, that his real legs were young, handsome and strong, but still he saw what he saw. Sometimes he even felt a sneaking admiration for the curse that had been placed on him. It had been long ago, in some village or other in the east. Or was it the west?

The emperor trailed his hand through the lukewarm water.

It had been a child's voice. Still a toddler, with a runny nose and eyes like sapphires.

"Why are they so ugly, Daddy?"

The emperor had seen immediately that the child was a witch.

"Imperial Emperors! I beg of you! She's just a child. My child! She doesn't know what she's saying! Please!"

That was clever, of course. A witch disguised as a child—a most cunning plan.

Later that night, he and his brother had stood on a hill and watched the village burn. There had been no witchcraft since then.

But the curse still remained.

He stared at his wrinkled arms, at the liver spots splashed across his hands like flecks of gravy. He pushed them deeper into the water, but he could still see them. Was it the heat that was making it more difficult than usual to keep his anxiety at bay?

When he finally drifted off into a parched half-sleep, a stream of memories came flowing over him. The mirror game he and his brother had played for their parents, with an empty gilded picture frame between them. His first horse, a pure-white Lipizzaner stallion, so spirited that he went tumbling from its back. His father, scarcely recognizable, on his deathbed.

Mother playing skittles with her friends, the tall golden bowling pins clattering as they toppled. And finally the image that concluded every dream: the monstrous emperor looming over him, his face full of terrifying holes and blemishes.

The emperor awoke with a start, his heart jerking and pounding in his chest. His cheeks were wet. Wet from the gherkin water, or had he been crying?

One of the buckets had fallen over. The gherkin water formed a thin layer on the marble floor. He did not dare to look at it.

"Brother?" he called softly. "Oh, brother?"

There was no reply.

The room, a hall so large that the bed was a postage stamp made of fabric, suddenly seemed cramped and stuffy, and the windows were black holes sucking out all the oxygen.

In spite of the heat, he shivered.

He opened the door and stood there for three minutes, perfectly still except for his hand, which had grasped the wall for support and was shaking so badly that the surface of the stone began to crumble.

"Brother?"

The soft, warm light of the torches illuminating the stone spiral staircase, the plush red stair carpet before him, the sweet sleep hanging in the castle's night air—stair by stair, they calmed him.

A song from long ago came into his head:

Where does the night go
when it is day?
Where must I look
when your smile fades away?
Where are the leaves
that fall from the trees?
Gone with the breeze.
Gone with the breeze.

Where is the ship
sunk in the waves?
Where are the lost
deep in their graves?
Where are the kisses
that nobody sees?
Gone with the breeze.
Gone with the breeze.

The song buzzed across his lips like a sad little bee. Curiously, he felt better. His cursed legs, usually as stiff and unbending as wooden poles, grew more flexible and powerful with every step. He was in such high spirits, in fact, that he did not even feel angry when he saw that the two guards who were supposed to be watching the entrance to the imperial chambers had dozed off.

Of course he would perform the roll call himself the next morning. He would roar that the One True Emperor had had a vision, that he had seen two pigs in the midst of his army, whose laziness was a direct attack on the One True Emperor's security. And he would ask them to make themselves known—before the One True Emperor did it for them.

Regardless of whether they immediately stepped forward or he had to unmask them, he meant to punish them.

A good whipping, the wheel of fire, or maybe filling two tubs to the brim with cow dung and leaving them in there for a couple of days while horseflies feasted on their fleshy faces.

He was a forgiving father.

By the dim light of dawn, the emperor came across the large shape in the middle of the library. He had no idea what the thing was or how it had got there. No one had informed him. The protocol for gifts to the emperor was that they were assessed and catalogued by the imperial steward, who then usually had them stored away in a room that was reserved for that purpose. But the steward was in the imperial palace, four hundred miles away, and although an official communication had gone from the lieutenant to the mayor of Vladzimka: "*Imperial gift from Blät to the emperor taken into custody at nine a.m. Awaiting further orders*," the message had not gone beyond the Blue Lamb, where the courier, a nervous man with chicken legs and a liking for gin, had peered through the inn's small window. As always, he was thirsty, but he was also careful. Two previous warnings about his drinking meant his job was already on the line and he did not want to run the risk of being spotted by anyone who might tell tales on him.

The courier leaned on the window ledge to get a better view. At that moment, he felt the wood give way beneath him. Shocked, he peered down between his hands and saw three tiny cracks zigzag across the brick.

There was a bang, followed by a quiet whooshing sound above and, when he looked up, the entire side wall of the Blue Lamb came tumbling down upon him.

It later emerged that the soldiers had, that very evening, sawn away one of the supports that the inn had rested upon for two centuries, to use for their own accommodation.

The emperor had no knowledge of any of this. He had by then discovered that the object was a cake, twelve feet high, and he pushed the wheeled library ladder over to the cake to take a closer look. He plucked a torch from one of the holders and then, step by step, he ventured up the steep, tall ladder. The smouldering torch had almost burned out and did not provide much light. Its shadowy, dancing glow moved across the gleaming red-and-white tiled floor, which had been polished only the evening before, and then fell on a line of letters, all lopsided and collapsing into the cake, which the emperor could make no sense of. An uneasy feeling came over him. For a moment, he considered waking one of the guards, but then he dismissed that idea.

Halfway up the steps, he remembered the third verse of the song from long ago.

The emperor did not know if it was really part of the song or had been added later. His mother had certainly never sung it. But the nanny who had nursed and looked after the twins sang it all the time.

Panting, the emperor climbed the last steps. The torch in his hand smoked and flickered for a moment before flaring as if in one final burst of strength. The rows of books all around the cake briefly revealed their dusty spines. The grey shadow of a mouse darted along an empty shelf. The white ceiling was covered with strange splashes of red.

But the emperor saw none of that.

His gaze was fixed on the cake.

He gasped.

Even in the enclosed space of the library, at the heart of the castle, the heat had finally seeped through the stones. And the cake, which had held out for so long, had finally given in.

What the emperor saw was worse than any nightmare.

Worse than the shattered porcelain emperor.

And far, far worse than any curse.

The grey wig of candyfloss had burst apart, leaving behind a bald and flaking scalp. The pink marzipan of the face had melted and merged with the sugar of the wig, turning it a sinister corpse-like hue. The cheeks of cherry juice had run and now resembled two deep, flesh-coloured wounds. What, less than two hours ago, had been a softly gleaming mouth of strawberry jelly, plump and pert, had now dried into a twisted sneer with crumbling peppermint teeth.

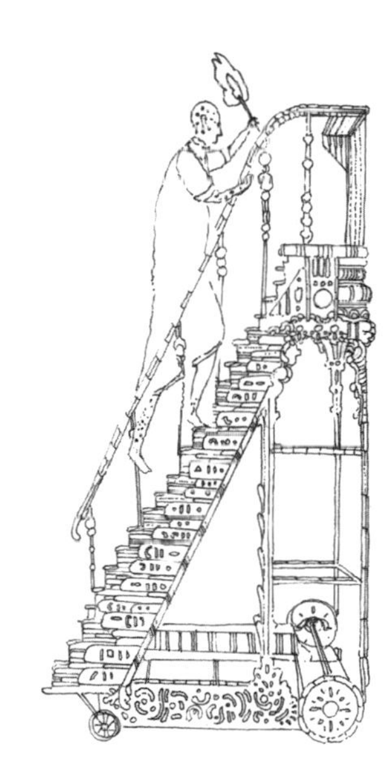

The eyes, the steel-blue boiled sweets, were terrifying. One appeared to be crawling with flies (the melted chocolate eyelashes) and the other had succumbed to gravity and begun a slow journey downwards.

At the point when the emperor saw it, the eye was halfway down the cheek; the sweet glistened as if it were crying and seemed so real in the flickering light that he was sure it was staring at him, straight into his soul.

With a greasy, blubbering sound, the cake imploded. The portrait split in two and began to sink.

And that was when the most terrifying moment came. From the cake, from its massive heart of cream, strawberry jelly and marzipan, came a loud, rattling groan. As if the shattered monster emperor himself, after years of silent protest at his banishment to the dungeons, were finally raising his voice.

The emperor also let out a cry, recoiled in panic, grabbed hold of the left-hand rail, only to realize the ladder had no left-hand rail, and then plummeted backwards, twelve feet down, onto the carefully polished tiled floor.

CHAPTER 28

Romantic fuss and nonsense

Tortot heard the bloodcurdling scream. Not long after that came the sound of hurried footsteps and shouted orders. The sounds echoed all around, outrunning one another, ricocheting off the walls of the corridors and doing an about-turn, all of which made it impossible to work out where they were coming from.

It sounded as if the entire army were in a state of alert.

Tortot stared at the maps, which, in his shock, he had dropped on the floor. There were only four of them left now. Four maps to find the final key, which led to the secret exit. Four maps that all looked alarmingly similar.

There was no time to work out which map was the right one. Turning back was not an option either. Without the previous maps, he would be hopelessly lost after just two turns. Tortot had no choice. He picked up the maps and chose the one on top. He ran down a corridor, took a side corridor on the right (which was correct), went down a flight of stairs (which was not on the map), passed through a courtyard with arches (that was right again). But the door that should have been at the rear of the courtyard was not there.

He heard boots running. Somewhere a halberd or some other weapon clattered to the floor, followed by curses.

Frantically, Tortot peered at the other sheets of paper. One of them also had a door on it, while the other two did not. Of those two, there was one map that led him back to a wooden throne halfway down the corridor where the voices now appeared to be coming from.

There was only one option left.

The last sheet of rice paper took him down the other side of the courtyard and up a flight of stairs, which was followed by a long, shadowy corridor with enormous tapestries on the wall.

The corridor turned out to be a dead end.

The voices were getting closer.

Tortot had no idea what had happened, but he did know one thing: the plan had failed.

Grimly, he stuffed the piece of paper into his mouth and took his cook's knife from his apron. He did not plan simply to surrender. He spied left into the dim corridor and was so focused on the attack that he paid no attention to the noise. When he heard it again and realized it was behind him, it was too late.

It was just as well he recognized the hand that clamped over his mouth, or the story could have turned out very differently.

Couraz did not say a word. She yanked Tortot back between two overlapping tapestries and into a shallow alcove. They stood motionless as the soldiers entered the corridor. There was confusion and men shouting orders back and forth. Tortot held his breath, scared that his panting belly would make the tapestry move in and out, giving away their position. He was sure his face had turned puce by the time Couraz indicated that the coast was clear.

She did not deem him worthy of a glance, but raced off, turning left, then right, so smoothly that Tortot wondered how often she had been here before. And why? "It wouldn't be the first time an informer was executed for being a double agent," she had said.

Did she mean that she?...

Tortot decided not to think too hard about that thought.

After lots of twists and turns, she came to a halt in a corridor where there was a writing cabinet. She held out her hand. In a strange reflex, he did the same. She stared at it, her eyebrows raised. He turned bright red.

"The last key," snapped Couraz.

The next moment, Couraz slid the cabinet aside to reveal a gate.

She opened the gate with the key. Behind it was a narrow entrance, barely big enough for a man to crawl through. But beyond that the corridor soon became wider and higher.

Daylight came surprisingly quickly. As Tortot emerged into the open air, he saw that they were less than two hundred yards from Vladzimka. The soldiers of Blät were ready and waiting.

"How did you know..." he began. "And how were you able to..."

"Men have to fight," was all that she replied. "But the planning's better left to women."

Her cart was there too, the halberd half-covered by a jumble of belongings.

"I don't know h... how to..." he began.

"Save your breath," said Couraz, as the soldiers marched past them, into the pitch-dark corridor, without making the slightest sound. "And make sure you get yourself and that boy out of the war."

"Maybe one day... when the war's over, we can... eh?" said Tortot. The worst thing was that Couraz let him go bumbling on. And when he had finished his awkward rambling, she laughed in his face.

He tried again. "But you said... You were the one who..."

"Drunken prattling," said Couraz. She flicked the reins and her horse trotted off.

The last he saw of her before she disappeared over the brow of the hill was her four-fingered hand. It was hard to say whether she was bidding him farewell or shooing an insect away. The halberd caught the light of the sun and glinted for a moment like a massive jewel.

Then she was gone and Tortot suddenly wondered to himself if maybe he liked romantic fuss and nonsense more than he would ever have imagined possible.

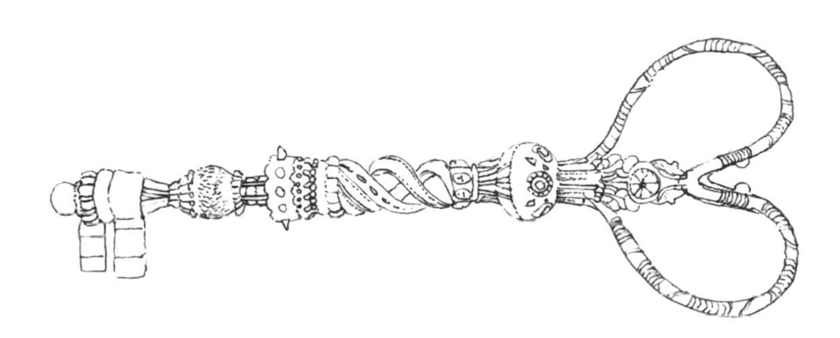

CHAPTER 29

In which the mincing machine turns one last time

In the entire history of the Wars of the Twin Emperors, including the War of the Gherkins, the fall of Vladzimka is still considered the fastest fall ever.

Contrary to what Tortot had believed, it was not the whole army that had been alerted by the emperor's cry. It was only the night watchmen and a few stray soldiers who had come within a hair's breadth of catching Tortot.

This meant that the troops of Blät were easily able to slip into the city through the secret corridor. They took the centre without a fight. By that time, the army of Vladzimka was in a state of alarm. Then Blät attacked the outer ring. And it must be said, as the Poker Player was later the first to admit: the army of Vladzimka offered fierce and organized resistance. It looked as if both armies would go on fighting to the last man.

At that point, the general was hiding with a few officers inside Vladzimka's tannery, among the large tubs where the leather lay soaking in urine. For the first time in his damaged life, the Poker Player was not afraid that other people would smell him.

In fact, he felt unusually relaxed. The prospect of leading a battle that would most probably enter the history books made him almost delighted. Even if he lost (which was not inconceivable), he would no longer go down in history as the general with the royal flush, or the general who had lost his half-army, which were rather dubious titles, but as the general who had employed an ingenious ruse to penetrate the fortress of Vladzimka. The only thing he regretted was that it would cost so many soldiers. The general was not a sentimental man, but he could appreciate a well-trained soldier, much as a farmer appreciates his horse or cow. It would be a shame to lose so much military capital in this battle.

So it is impossible to say if he felt relieved or disappointed when, in the brooding silence of the approaching confrontation, the enemy suddenly raised a commotion. At first, he steeled himself—noise from the enemy did not usually bode well—until he heard what they were shouting.

He's dead!
The emperor's dead!
He's broken his neck!

During the frantic, hurried summit meeting between Blät and Vladzimka, the city's plight soon became clear: without an emperor, it was uncertain whether the counties (who had first taken the side of Blät and then the side of Vladzimka) would continue to support the city of Vladzimka or would take Blät's side once again. The Poker Player, at the pinnacle of his diplomatic skills, presented a third scenario: the counties would become a third party in the war, independent of any emperor, and the first victory they claimed would be Vladzimka. And everyone knew what kind of cruel, ruthless scoundrels the counties produced.

Less than four hours after the attack had begun, Vladzimka surrendered.

Tortot had been ordered to await the outcome by the secret entrance. He sat on a tree trunk, whittling a stick with his knife, as a slow stream of men flowed in and out of the corridor.

Soldiers sat around, playing cards. A hussar had hung his army coat in the branches of an elm tree and was taking a nap. It was then that Tortot thought once again how surprisingly similar war could seem to peace, and vice versa.

And that was also when he received news of Crookleg's death.

To this day, historians are still puzzled about what exactly happened. Crookleg had been given the emperor on a platter, hadn't he? Surely all he had to do was overpower him? A weak old man with a heart condition would have been no match for the hulking sergeant, even with his shrinking leg and his granite-heeled limp.

So where had it gone wrong?

One theory says that the sergeant, in spite of his enthusiasm for his own plan, was overcome by sleep. And when he awoke with a shock, he had not remembered where he was and he must have panicked.

Another theory assumed that he had not fallen asleep at all, but had waited for the emperor, and when he had heard him (or maybe even smelled him, given the pungent scent of gherkins that always accompanied the emperors), he had taken a step back to shoot out through the concealed hatch, which was when it had all gone wrong.

A third theory was based instead on the weak frame of the compartment within the cake and the sheer weight of all those hundreds of gallons of cream, marzipan, chocolate and sweets.

Whatever had happened, though, it turned out disastrously for the sergeant.

The twelve-foot-high peace offering collapsed on Crookleg.

Under normal circumstances, other than a nasty, slimy shower of rancid ingredients, that would have had few serious consequences. But, precisely because of the weight of the massive cake, the dish it was resting on had been constructed of thick glazed tiles on a metal frame. And whether it was the sergeant's frantic attempts to free himself or simply the sheer weight of the cake, the boot with the granite heel had plunged through the glazed tiles and become stuck in the frame.

As a result, Crookleg had become the first and only sergeant in the long history of the Wars of the Twin Emperors, including the War of the Gherkins, to drown in a cake during combat.

"I understand from General Nilliewasser that it was your idea to lay siege to Vladzimka by presenting them with a cake as a peace offering?" asked the mayor of Blät, a man with teeth like an ancient horse's.

No one was quite sure where he and his entourage had appeared from. For most of the siege, the mayor had barely shown his face, but now he was suddenly there before Tortot, polished and gleaming like an apple.

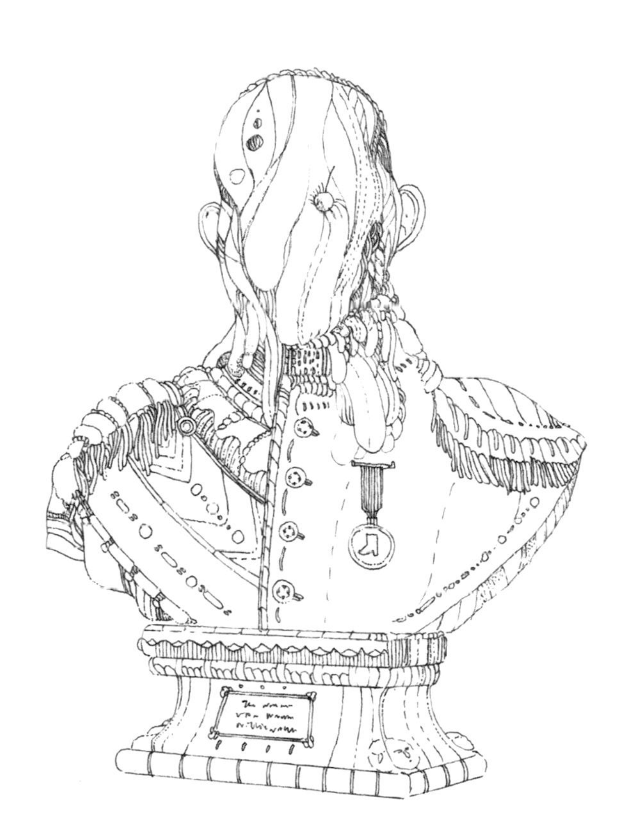

The Poker Player stood beside the mayor.

There was a small trickle of curious onlookers, but few of the soldiers seemed very interested in the mayor's arrival on the battlefield—much to the obvious displeasure of the mayor himself.

"That was you?"

Tortot glanced at the Poker Player. His expression was blank, but when he felt Tortot's eyes on him, he gave a brief cough.

"That was you?" repeated the mayor.

Tortot nodded.

"Then, in light of recent events, I am delighted to inform you, without further ado, that it pleases the emperor, the Only Remaining and One True Emperor, to reward you amply, most copiously..."—at this point the mayor gasped for breath, his horsey teeth clattering noisily—"... with the Cross of Merit for Courage and Dauntlessness, and it further pleases the emperor that you should accept his invitation to express your heart's desire, so that, in His Infinite Generosity and Wisdom, he can bring your wish to fruition and..."

"Yes, that's very nice," said Tortot, interrupting him, "but if you'll excuse me now, I spent the night inside a cake, so I'd like to freshen up a little. And besides, I need to inspect my supplies, because what with all the memorials and commemorations that are being planned..."

And he left the stunned mayor standing there as he pushed his way through the soldiers and raced down the hill, along the path of skulls to Blät.

The city gate was open for the first time in two years. The entire population of Blät seemed to have left the city. People were splashing and swimming in the castle moat, couples were kissing and cuddling in the fields, children ran through the meadows, their excited voices echoing off the half-collapsed city walls. The old people strolled to the cemetery and sighed as they began to

repair the damage of overturned gravestones, defaced tombs and one enormous rosebush that had run rampant over everything.

In the city itself, all was quiet. Here and there, a drunkard sat sleeping off the drink. From the makeshift village of tarpaulin and scrap came the snoring of soldiers who were trying to dream the war out of their heads.

The courtyard and the convent itself were still half in shadow; only the bell tower was bathed in bright sunlight.

Tok-Bong! Tok-Bong!

Tortot quietly opened the kitchen door and stood there for a moment.

A slanting ray of morning light shone in through one of the windows.

The oven sparkled, the pans and knives hung gleaming in their ranks, the chopping boards were in a neat formation on the table, you could eat off the floor, and there was not one single splash or stain.

Tortot had a strange feeling of homesickness, as if he were already thousands of miles away with only a memory of this place.

He called himself to order. No time for sentimental nonsense. Action!

He took off his apron, oiled his cook's knife and slid it back into the block.

He removed his jerkin, which was covered in sweat and cream, and filled a bucket with water so that he could freshen up.

"Wake up," he said to the gherkin barrel. "Come on, sleepyhead, open your eyes. The day is drawing on. And what a day it is!"

There was a long, soft moan.

"Yes, yes," said Tortot, "the night is full of dreams wanting to be dreamed, but that's no reason to lie sleeping. You like stories, don't you? Well, I have a story for you. Such a magnificent story! Those brothers of yours would be green with envy if they heard it. They'd think: How in God's name is it possible that we didn't think up that story? Don't we have any imagination at all? Don't we keep our eyes and ears open at all times? Well, it's that kind of story!"

Tortot leaned forward and plunged his face into the cool water. He had never known water could feel so good on your skin, it seemed not only to be washing away the sticky cream from his eyebrows and the sweat from his neck, but also as if all those wars were streaming away and dissolving.

"It's a story that deserves a title," said Tortot, "not one that you can just launch into without knowing if anyone's listening. Maybe you'll come up with a title for me later, but for now I'm calling it: 'How the Great Tortot Conquered Vladzimka with the Help of the Brilliant Cake Ruse.' How does that sound?"

Waking up is a hard thing to do when you are young. All Tortot heard was a quiet scratching. He took it for a "yes".

And he told the story. He told it in all its colourful details. Tortot had never been a man for stories, even the smallest of jokes defeated him after just a couple of words. But now one word followed the next, like a long unbroken string of sausages. How cramped it had been inside the cake, and Crookleg's sweat, truly unbelievable! Oh, and he'd completely forgotten to tell him that the sergeant...

no, really, Half-George! And how Couraz had suddenly been there, and how she had blindly... and the pitch-dark corridor, really, not a hand in front of your face, even a blind man never had that much darkness inside his head, it was as if the darkness crept into you, and nothing of yourself remained, and you could barely remember ever having had a body, so that, when you reached the end, you were startled to see your hand suddenly there and you thought it was a huge spider and...

There was a yawn. For a moment, Tortot was offended, but then he remembered that Half-George had probably had hardly a wink of sleep in the heat of the night. And a story was, after all, just a story. What counted, what it was really about, was what good that story did you.

"The Emperor's Cross of Merit, honorary citizenship of Vladzimka, a bunch of certificates of recognition, you know, it wouldn't surprise me if they gave us a nice big bag of money too, but that's not the point, lad. Do you know what we're going to do? Do you know? We're going to get out of the war game. You and me. We're going to a place that's past the war. What do you say to that?"

It was quiet inside the barrel now. Of course it was quiet. What would he have done himself if his dearest wish had suddenly come true? He would not have immediately jumped for joy either, would he? First he would have thought: How? Why?

So Tortot told him about the wish.

"I shall ask the emperor to give me and the gherkin barrel an escort to my village. And the first thing we'll do when we get there is burn this stinking old barrel. And if we can't find any barrels left in the village, I'll have a new one made. Which would be better anyway. This barrel has had its day. If we get one made, we'll be able to decide the measurements ourselves. I'll order a barrel for you, my boy, a barrel as big as a house. You won't believe your eyes. There'll be a sitting room downstairs, and a kitchen. And a little bedroom upstairs with a round bed. But it'll have to be a bit of a crooked barrel, of course, because otherwise it won't fit in, you know."

There was a quiet whine.

Tortot had had enough. He strode over to the barrel, lifted the lid and, the next moment, a reddish-brown shadow slipped out. The convent cat leaped silently onto the floor, took a few steps, sat down, wrapped its tail around itself, yawned, looked at the barrel and then began to meow, loud and mournfully.

Tortot glanced into the barrel.
Frowned.
And stood there.
And stood there.
And leaned forward a little.
And reached out his hand.
And felt.
And gasped and stepped back.
And stood there.
And felt again.
And took a deep breath.
And stood there.
And stood there.
And stood there.
Sat down.
Stood up again.
And then closed the lid.
Very carefully.

He took his cook's knife, a handful of onions, and sat down on a stool beside the barrel. "But that's not all," he said. "Do you know what I thought of, my boy? Do you know what else I thought of, when I was sitting inside the cake? I suddenly remembered the watchmaker in the town two days' walk from the village. Did you know he's not just a watchmaker but also an inventor? He'll make new legs for you, Half-George. He'll make a *whole* George out of you again. I shall say to him: Now listen here, my good man. These can't be just any old legs. Money is not an issue. They need to have a mechanism that'll let you walk again, and even hop. And they'll have a button that you can press to make you walk so elegantly that all the girls will turn their heads. And all the boys will be envious. They'll dream that they were cut in half too. What am I saying? Being halved will become the latest fashion."

The words kept on coming; he had not known he had so many. He spoke them, he felt the sounds passing through his lips, but he had no idea what he was saying.

"Tortot! Tortot!"
"What?"
"So everything's crooked, eh?"
"Where?"
"In your village."
"Where did you get that idea from?"
"You dream at night. Out loud."

But it is possible that he did not say a single word. That it was all just noises.

"Tortot! Tortot!"
"What now?"
"My feet hurt."
"You don't even have feet anymore."
"I know, but my feet don't seem to care about that."

Or maybe he made no sound at all. That was also a possibility. Maybe his lips were moving, but the sounds were all inside his head. And if someone came in, they would see the cook sitting beside the barrel, his lips moving, but even if they held their ear close to those lips, they still would not hear a sound.

"I'd believe it if you promised me something, Tortot."

"But I won't do that."

"I could rest easy."

"I'm not promising you anything, Half-George, not even a grain of salt."

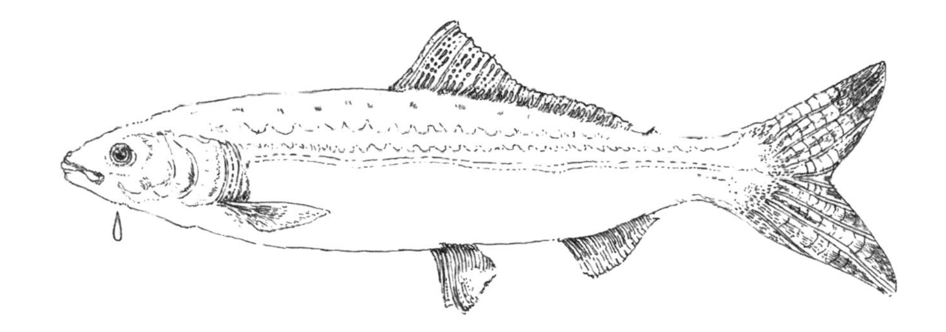

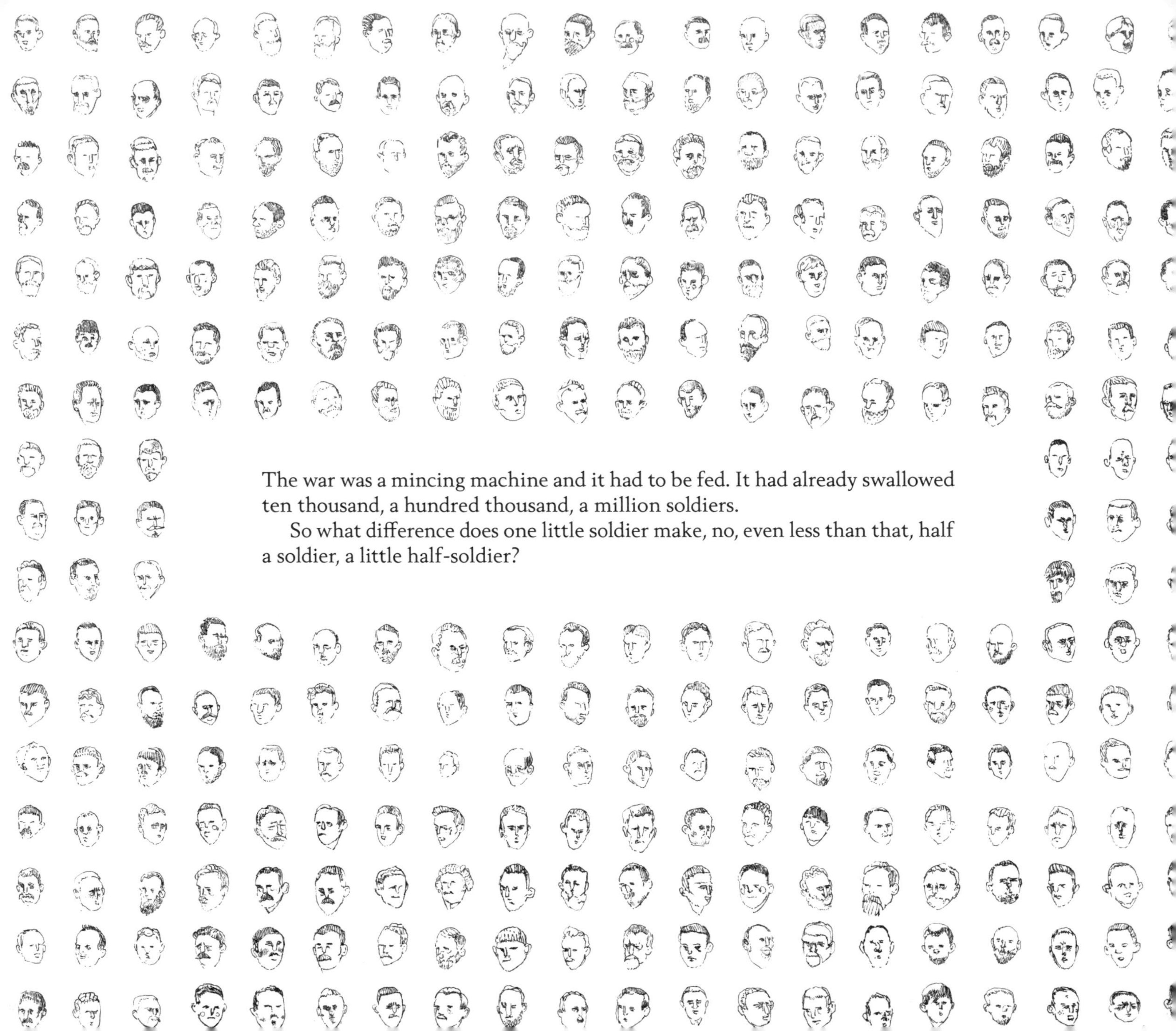

The war was a mincing machine and it had to be fed. It had already swallowed ten thousand, a hundred thousand, a million soldiers.

So what difference does one little soldier make, no, even less than that, half a soldier, a little half-soldier?

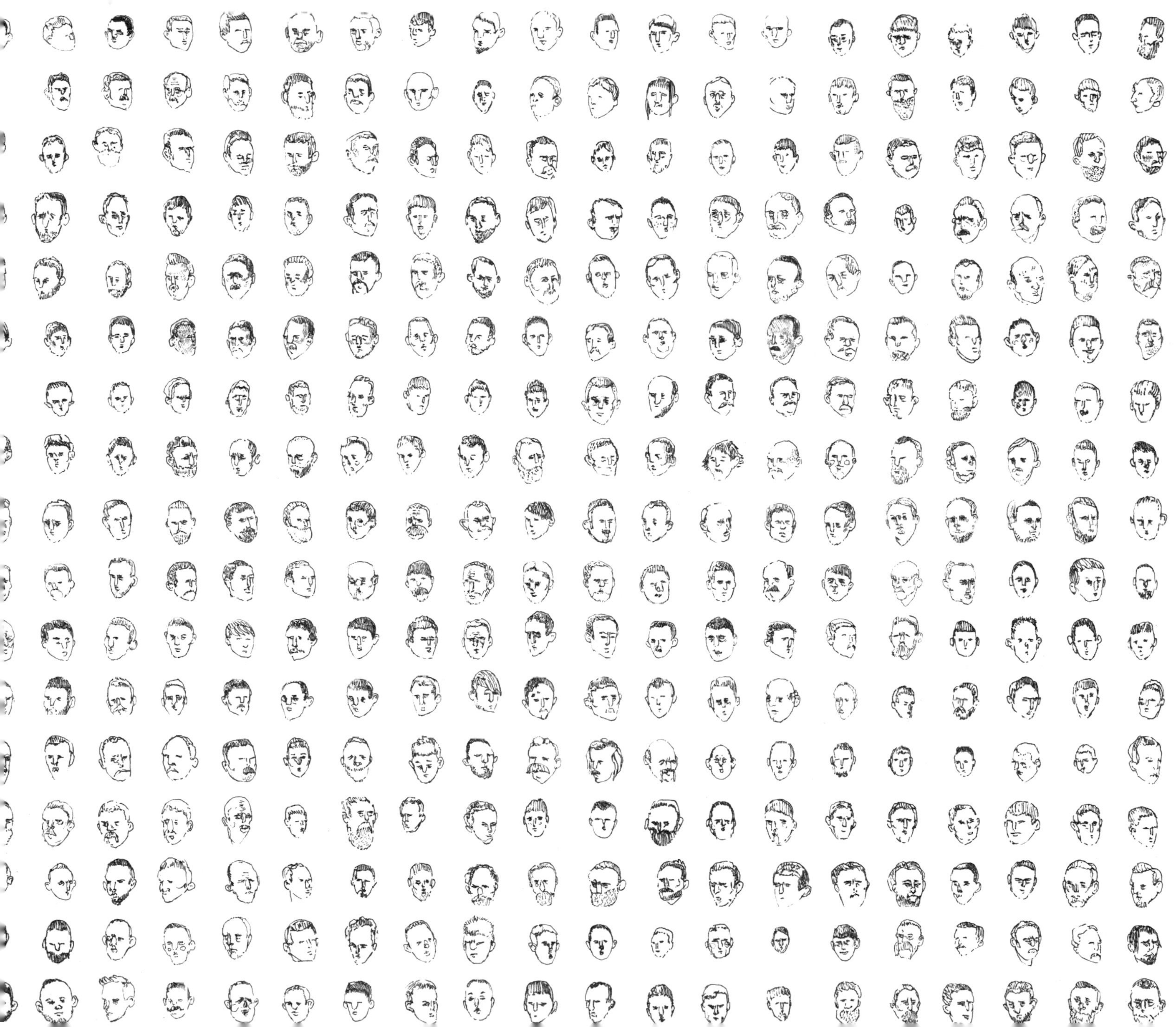

One little half-soldier was insignificant.

CHAPTER 30
Tortot's wish

One sunny morning, a funeral procession made its way out of Blät. Three drummers led the way, beating a slow, sad rhythm. They were followed by the donkey cart with Tortot sitting up front, flanked by an honour guard of officers.

That evening, it was the subject on everyone's lips.

"Only officers?"

"Yes."

"No sergeant-majors or privates?"

"Only officers."

The procession walked for half a day. The flat landscape became hillier. In the distance they could see the river, a twisting grey-green snake that wanted to slither away, but never went anywhere. They walked and walked, until the cook, who all that time had been peering around as if he had lost his nose, suddenly drove the cart into a half-hidden field.

The rye was waist-high. The drummers, who continued along the road until they realized that the cook had taken a different direction, hurried after him into the field and tried to take the lead again. They struggled to march in step and had to force their big drums through the rye. Sometimes an officer stumbled. The tight rhythm grew shaky, and it all became so difficult (the cook kept looking around, walking to the east, then the west, then from north to south) that the drummers eventually stopped drumming altogether. The increasingly disorganized honour guard kept giving one another bewildered looks, but no one dared to say anything. The Poker Player had made it clear: "I couldn't care less how potty the cook's wish might sound. Not a peep, or you'll lose a month's pay."

Finally, the cook found what he was looking for.

The chaplain blessed the gherkin barrel. And then muttered something that sounded less like a prayer, and more like "rhubarbrhubarbrhubarb".

The cook did not seem to care. He watched as the officers unloaded spades from the cart and began to dig.

"Can you imagine? They had clods of mud all the way up to their powdered wigs. But that's not all."

"Really?"

"The barrel was given a full military salute and a reveille. And the Cross of Merit for Courage and Dauntlessness."

"No!"

"And if you think that was the end of it... All the officers had to walk back in their socks."

"What?"

"I swear it. They had to leave their boots behind on the grave. Polished to a shine and with tassels and all."

CHAPTER 31
What mothers are made of

Less than a month after Keflavik (or Husavik) had broken his neck falling down the library ladder, Husavik (or Keflavik) climbed out of bed one sunny morning, stretched, walked stiffly to the window of his castle tower, stepped outside, and fell forty feet. It has never been established if he did it absent-mindedly or if it was one last, deliberate mirror game, but he lay in a coma for two weeks and then quietly died.

This brought fifty years of warmongering to an abrupt end.

Soon after that, the first ladies and gentlemen arrived with their suitcases, binoculars and travel guides.

You could walk the corridors of the palace and view the bedroom where the Twin Emperors had slept—and the tubs in which the gherkin jelly was heated. Visitors could shudder at the sight of the monstrous porcelain emperor.

Also available for purchase in a handy pocket size from our shop at the exit!!

As the attraction proved so popular, the newly established tourist office designated no fewer than four hovels as the "hut where the Twin Emperors caught smallpox".

And Tortot?

The day he left the army for good, he planned to roam the world, to get lost, to disappear. And although he allowed his bespectacled donkey to walk on without any plan, he was not really surprised when, one golden afternoon, with the sun still hanging lazily above the horizon, he heard a quiet little thud-thud-thudding

sound. When he looked up, it felt as if he were seeing the world for the first time: the crooked wall that the donkey was rubbing its rump against, the crooked tree in the middle of the crooked garden, and the lizards falling asleep and rolling onto the ground, where they lay dozing.

As if in a dream, he tied up his bespectacled donkey.

She could so easily not have been there. Mothers are made of sons. And when those sons are no longer there, they might as well not be there either.

But the herbs in the garden were growing thick and green. Her shawl lay on the crooked bench beneath the crooked oak.

And her shoes with the swivel heel were by the back door. From the house, her voice sang:

Herbs, herbs,
so green and so good,
flourishing, nourishing,
grow as you should.
Stretch out your shoots,
push down your roots.
Flourish and swell,
nourish us well.
Herbs, herbs,
so good and so green,
nourishing, flourishing,
the finest I've seen.
Herbs, herbs,
please grow like spring,
thrive, look alive,
and make my heart sing.

She did not ask him anything when she saw him. She did not say anything either.
And he did not have to tell her anything.

But he told her anyway.